"Go ahead,"

Sarah said, and inexplicably proud, she put his hand on her belly. "There."

His fingers were warm and strong, and Sarah was jolted by the feelings that his touch set off within her.

The baby wiggled, and Steve's mouth dropped open a little. The baby kicked, and Steven's eyes flashed up to meet Sarah's. Then the baby really got going, producing a short series of rapid-fire punches, and Steve laughed with wonder and joy.

So did Sarah.

Then the laughter died and the baby stopped moving. Steve seemed reluctant, but removed his hand. "Wow," he said. "That was something."

Dear Reader,

Happy Spring! It's May, the flowers are blooming and love is in the air. It's the month for romance—both discovery and renewal—the month for mothers and the time of new birth. It's a wonderful time of year!

And in this special month, we have some treats in store for you. Silhouette Romance's DIAMOND JUBILEE is in full swing, and *Second Time Lucky* by Victoria Glenn is bound to help you get into the springtime spirit. Lovely heroine Lara discovers that sometimes love comes from unexpected sources when she meets up with handsome, enigmatic Miles. Don't miss this tender tale! Then, in June, *Cimarron Knight*, the first book in Pepper Adams's exciting new trilogy—*CIMARRON STORIES*—will be available. Set on the plains of Oklahoma, these three books are a true delight.

The DIAMOND JUBILEE—Silhouette Romance's tenth anniversary celebration—is our way of saying thanks to you, our readers. To symbolize the timelessness of love, as well as the modern gift of the tenth anniversary, we're presenting readers with a DIAMOND JUBILEE Silhouette Romance title each month, penned by one of your favorite Silhouette Romance authors. In the coming months writers such as Marie Ferrarella, Lucy Gordon, Dixie Browning, Phyllis Halldorson—to name just a few—are writing DIAMOND JUBILEE titles especially for you.

And that's not all! Laurie Paige has a heartwarming duo coming up—*Homeward Bound*. The first book, *A Season for Homecoming*, is coming your way in June. Peggy Webb also has *Venus de Molly*, a sequel to *Harvey's Missing*, due out in July. And much-loved Diana Palmer has some special treats in store during the months ahead....

I hope you'll enjoy this book and all of the stories to come. Come home to romance—Silhouette Romance—for always!

Sincerely,
Tara Hughes Gavin
Senior Editor

MELODIE ADAMS

In the
Family Way

Published by Silhouette Books New York

America's Publisher of Contemporary Romance

For my husband, Steve,
and our precious new daughter, Alexandra,
with love

SILHOUETTE BOOKS
300 E. 42nd St., New York, N.Y. 10017

ISBN: 0-373-08722-5

First Silhouette Books printing May 1990

Printed in the U.S.A.

MELODIE ADAMS

spent her childhood years in various states west of the Mississippi, and claims that it was "a terrific, ever-changing, always interesting way to grow up." Still, in spite of all the wonderful places she's seen, Melodie's favorite way to relax is to spend a day in the sun, a tall glass of iced tea in one hand and a good romance in the other.

Lake Michigan

ILLINOIS

Des Plaines

Wilmette

Evanston

Oak Park

Cicero

Chicago

CHICAGO AND VICINITY

Chapter One

She had been expecting him for the last couple of days. Now, here he stood, in her tiny cubicle of an office, in all his tanned, manly glory.

His height—at least six two, had not been exaggerated, nor had his looks, which office gossip had likened to Robert Redford's. The hair was similar, Sarah thought, studying him critically. Sandy blond, thick, sun streaked and finger combed. The strong line of jaw and straight cut of nose struck a familiar chord. And there was something about the eyes, pale and penetrating, although this man's were an odd shade of mintish green rather than Redford's blue.

He wore an unconstructed, tan linen suit and the white, easy smile that had risen to rapid fame among the women at Houston Publishing.

"Hi," he said, laugh lines crinkling around those strange green eyes. "I hope I'm not interrupting. I'm Steve Carlisle. I'm the—"

"Yes," Sarah said, tucking a section of straight, dark brown hair behind her ear. "I know who you are. The consultant Mark brought in to save our sinking ship."

"To *help* save it," he said with the charming modesty Sarah had also heard about. "I'm just a part of the team."

He smiled again and came farther into the office, obviously intending to stay and chat for a while. Which, according to the office grapevine, was all he'd done for the last two days since he'd arrived— chat, flirt and joke around with everyone from vice presidents to janitors to secretaries and copy editors, and talk about everything under the sun except Houston Publishing and its problems.

An incredible, inexcusable waste of time. According to Mark Donovan, they needed to move quickly to pull Houston's back up to snuff. A relatively small company, it couldn't afford to sustain itself for long without some of the little perks one comes to depend upon in business—like profits.

"And you are," Steve said, moving to the wall opposite her desk and leaning casually against it, "the famous Miss Sarah Jordan, editor *extraordinaire*, according to Mark Donovan."

"Editor in chief," she said, and hoped her tone of voice informed him of her immunity to flattery. She had been charmed—and conned—by the best, and had no intentions of ever letting it happen again.

"Ah, yes," he said. "Editor in chief. Sorry. I haven't had a chance to sit down and study your magazine yet, but Mark tells me it's very good."

"We work hard," Sarah said, getting impatient. Maybe hotshot consultants had time for small talk, but she did not. Especially now.

She leaned forward, nearly hidden behind the piles of manuscripts and file folders on her desk. "What can I help you with, Mr. Carlisle?"

Her briskness got through. He straightened from the wall.

"Well," he said, and shrugged. "Nothing really. Yet. Actually, I just stopped by to meet you and say hello—for now. At this point I'm trying to get a general overview of things, then I'll be scheduling time with people from all the departments to discuss specific situations and possible alternative courses of..."

Gibberish, Sarah thought, barely listening. To cover up for wasting time.

After all, a consultant's expenses were paid. Car and accommodations supplied. And knowing Mark Donovan, the pay and fringe benefits were generous, especially since Golden Boy here was Mark's nephew.

Her mouth tightened, lips pressing into a straight line to keep from frowning.

He talked on, saying nothing.

She half listened, while the other part of her mind returned to work, checking off what she'd accomplished and what still had to be done that day. They were getting ready to go to press on the October issue, and it still had to be proofed. She had five articles to go over and eight new proposals to read. There was an editorial meeting right after lunch... and it was 12:05 now. Fifty-five minutes to herself. And out of that she desperately needed a thirty-minute nap.

Naps! Ridiculous, time-eating things reserved for babies. And these days, for Sarah.

Prior to this year, Sarah had never taken a *nap* in her life. Yet now, when she needed to accomplish more than ever, naps were an infuriating necessity. If she skipped the one at noon, she dragged through the rest of the day, getting far less done than her goal schedule allowed. If she skipped the one before dinner, her evening was shot. So she surrendered, and took naps.

And she needed one now.

Another glance at the black-and-white, institution-style wall clock nudged her habitual fatigue.

A yawn formed; she tried to smother it. Failed.

Steven Carlisle stopped talking, trailing off in midsentence.

"Excuse me," Sarah said, and blinked, forcing alertness, forcing politeness. "Please go on, Mr. Carlisle. You were saying?"

He'd been frowning, looking both perplexed and irritated at her obvious lack of fascination with his presence. He shook his head.

"Doesn't matter," he said. "Nothing important. To tell you the truth, I was getting a little bored with the spiel myself."

More modesty. How very charming.

"I wasn't bored, Mr. Carlisle. Just tired. It sort of goes with the territory for me right now. I apologize for being rude."

"Not at all," he said. Then a teasing smile. "I just hope you're not so tired because old Mark's been working you too hard. Rumor has it he's a pain in the neck to work for."

"Your uncle is a wonderful man, Mr. Carlisle. A fine human being and a fair and caring employer. We're all very eager to do what we can in the revitalization plans for Houston's. That is, of course, as soon as a plan is formed...."

An edge to her last words made them a challenge. *Get to work!* that statement shouted. *Quit messing around, Golden Boy, and show us your stuff! If, of course, you've got any stuff....*

His green eyes narrowed.

It was gratifyingly obvious that her message had been received, loud and clear.

"Well," he said, and offered a tight smile, "I'm glad to know I can count on your help. I'm sure you're very busy, so I won't keep you any longer, Miss—is it Miss?" he asked. "Or Mrs.?" His glance moved downward, looking for rings.

Sarah eyed him steadily, disliking him more and more.

"It's Ms.," she said. Which told him absolutely nothing except that her marital status—or *anything* personal about her—was none of his business.

"I see," he said, holding her gaze.

"I'm glad." She made herself smile. "It was very nice meeting you, Mr. Carlisle. Thank you for stopping by. Do let me know the minute you've got something for me to do to help with your plans."

He nodded. "I'll do that, Ms. Jordan. That is, of course, as soon as a plan is formed."

Sarah watched him leave, then closed her eyes and shook her head.

Men, she thought, and left it at that. Sometimes a single word could pretty well say it all.

She sighed and moved a stack of manuscripts to the edge of her desk, making a place to prop her feet. As always, she felt irritated at sacrificing valuable work time to sleep, but she had no option. Her body was no longer her own. Some automatic pilot had switched on many months ago and taken control.

She closed her eyes, and then, of course, a knock sounded at her door.

Diane Fitzgerald poked her blond head inside the office.

"Well?" the woman asked. "Have you met him yet?"

The rest of Diane's body followed—a slim, light body that Sarah envied right now.

She pushed away from her desk and absently rubbed the bulging mound of her own stomach, comparing it to the flatness of Diane's. Hard to believe that she and this woman had once traded clothes.

"Yes, I met him. You just missed him. He left a minute or two ago."

There was no point in pretending she didn't know who the woman was talking about. Steven Carlisle was all *anyone* had talked about for the last two days.

"And...?" Diane prompted, settling her tall, willowy frame into an extra chair.

"And what?" Sarah frowned, irritated that she had to waste even more time on Steven Carlisle.

Diane shrugged. "What did you think? Isn't he gorgeous?"

"Yes," Sarah said, wanting to grind her teeth. "He is. But Diane, good looks and charm do not a good business consultant make. I have a bad feeling about him. I told you that right from the start. Meeting him didn't change it."

"Surprise, surprise," Diane murmured dryly.

"Meaning?" Sarah's expression challenged.

"Never mind," the blonde said. "But let the record show that I think he's going to prove to be a brilliant businessman."

"How can you say that? He's done nothing around here but flirt with the female population for two days! You watch, Diane. The man is all show and no go. I know his type. *Everyone* knows his type."

"Mark Donovan is no fool," Diane said. "He wouldn't have hired him if—"

"If he hadn't been his nephew," Sarah said. "I think Mark was simply blinded by family loyalty— but I do hope I'm wrong. I'd like nothing better than for Golden Boy Carlisle to prove *me* the fool and come up with something brilliant to help Houston's."

"Golden Boy?" Diane raised an eyebrow.

Sarah grinned. "Seems to suit him, doesn't it?"

"Not the way you say it. I swear, Sarah, you can pack more sarcasm into a couple of words than anybody I've ever known."

Sarah laughed. "What can I say? It's a gift."

She stopped talking because she had to yawn. In front of Diane, there was no need to hide her fatigue.

"Oh, what I would do for a nap," Sarah said, and yawned again. She smiled at her friend. "You don't mind if I run you off, do you? I've got a heavy afternoon and a meeting at one."

"Say no more." The blonde stood up, studied Sarah and her expression clouded with concern. "Are you feeling okay?"

Sarah grinned sleepily. "No, I'm feeling pregnant. Which is not the same as feeling okay. But other than that, yeah, I'm great."

"You're sure." Diane peered at her, obviously trying to decipher the truth.

"Yes, I'm sure." Sarah shook her head and put her feet up on a carton of manuscripts she still had to find time to get through. "Look at this." She wiggled her feet—and changed the subject. "My ankles are about twice their normal size. Disgusting, isn't it?"

"Not as disgusting as having one be fat and one skinny, which I had when I was carrying Jana."

"You're kidding."

"I'm not," Diane said. "And it was summer, so my ankles showed. And people stared."

Sarah laughed, both at the story and Diane's wry, wide-eyed expression. "I guess I have something to be grateful for then, don't I?" She looked at her matching sausage ankles again.

"You better believe it," Diane said, starting toward the door. "Oh, before I go, I wanted to ask if you've checked on the classes. Time is running out, you know."

"Mmm." Sarah looked at her hands, fingers swollen and ringless, nails short, clean and unpolished. She picked absently at a cuticle. "There's a new session starting next week. Tuesdays or Thursdays. But, Diane . . . I've been thinking. I appreciate your offer to be my coach, but I really don't need a coach. I talked to the nurse at my o.b.'s office yesterday, and she says I don't absolutely have to have someone. The labor nurses can coach me along."

Diane's lips pursed. "Are you saying you don't want me to be your coach?"

Sarah picked up a pen and doodled on her desk-pad. "I'm saying that I can handle this alone."

"You'd rather?" Diane challenged, her voice soft.

Sarah met her eyes. "I'm just saying that it's unnecessary to have someone there. They won't let you in if you haven't taken the classes, and the classes are going to take up a lot of time. I just don't see the point."

And Diane had her own family to worry about. Sarah didn't want to impose. She only wished she hadn't accepted Diane's generous offer in the first place—before taking time to think about all it entailed.

Labor was not a pretty experience, for the mother or the coach. It could last twenty or thirty hours and was grueling, emotionally and physically. She had already been warned that mothers yelled and screamed and cussed their doctors, nurses, coaches...anyone in the vicinity. When the coach was your husband and you were in it together, that was one thing. But when the coach was a caring friend, expecting her to endure the whole ordeal was quite another.

"It's a few hours once a week," Diane said, frowning. "I think I can spare it, even for something so trivial as my friend having a baby. Come on, Sarah. Don't play noble about this. Childbirth is no time for a woman to be alone."

"No," Sarah said decisively. "I appreciate the offer, but I really think this is something I want to handle myself. Besides—" she smiled to change the mood "—the way I hear it, when you're in labor, you aren't aware of anybody else, anyway. Everybody I've talked to tells me you just keep screaming *'Knock me out! Just knock me out!'* And all your noble plans for natural childbirth go right down the tubes."

Diane laughed. "Does ring a bell, actually. Things can get pretty intense. But that's only at the end, Sarah. The rest isn't so bad. It's just *long.* You need somebody there to talk to, watch TV with, walk the halls with. Somebody to talk you through the contractions and help distract you in between." Her eyes were earnest. "Sarah, I really want to be there."

Sarah swallowed, really *wanting* her to be there and hating herself for the weakness that kept trying to prevent her from doing the right thing.

"Let's talk about it later," she said. "Okay? Right now, I'm so tired I can't even think."

Diane hesitated, clearly wanting to argue the point. But when Sarah put her feet on her desk and leaned back in her creaky swivel chair, the blonde gave in.

"See you later," Diane said. "Call if you need anything—even if it's only a glass of water."

"I will," Sarah said.

And they both knew that that was a lie.

Across the table, Jeri McFadden laughed, her green eyes sparkling with mischief and light flirtatiousness as she finished telling a tale of confusion at forty-thousand feet. Five nine, leggy, with a fabulous, kinky mane of fiery-red hair, Jeri was a flight attendant Steve had met on the plane to Chicago. He'd flirted with her and she'd flirted back, and at the time he had thought she might be the ideal occasional companion to brighten his stay while he sorted out Houston's problems. They'd made a lunch date and Steve had been looking forward to it.

Yet . . . now that he was here, he couldn't seem to keep his mind on the conversation. Or his companion. He was looking at Jeri and seeing Sarah Jordan—that straight, silky fall of black-brown hair, long bangs that nearly touched thick, black lashes.

And those eyes, those huge eyes, the deep, warm, rich color of espresso....

Fabulous.

That had been his first thought when he'd walked through her door.

And then the chemistry had hit. Hard. That little zinging sensation that goes from your head to your toes and charges all your nether regions.

That kind of instant, jolting, chemical reaction to a woman hadn't happened to him in a long, long time.

To tell the truth, it had surprised him so much, that he'd felt a little shaken. But he'd been very careful not to let any of his reactions show.

In fact, he'd been so concerned with holding his own feelings that it had taken him several minutes to realize something that should have hit him right at the outset.

Sarah Jordan did not feel that same, instantaneous kind of chemistry and attraction. Yet, it wasn't something so simple and innocuous as an understandable indifference to a total stranger. For some reason, Sarah Jordan really did *not* like him at *all*. *Dis*liked him, as a matter of fact. In the space of those few, hard-hitting minutes, she had managed to make that perfectly clear.

A dilemma. To say the very least.

Because high-voltage attractions like that were so very rare, you couldn't just walk away without at least an attempt at pursuing it to see where it went.

Yet . . . when the lady was just not interested—

"Steve," Jeri said, demanding his attention. "I'm sorry to cut this short, but I've really got to go." She glanced at her watch and slid across the banquette.

Feeling guilty for his lack of attention, Steve jumped up and took her elbow. "I'll run you out to the airport."

"Thanks," she said. "You're a doll. But I've got a ride. A pilot friend. He's picking me up out front." Smiling, she pressed him back down onto the seat. "Stay. Have that second cup of coffee I'm going to have to miss. Enjoy." She gave him a swift, sweet kiss, thanked him for the lunch, told him to call. And then she was gone.

And Steve was alone. With his dilemma.

He started to rise and leave, then decided to take Jeri's advice and settled back in.

He had some thinking to do about the plans for Houston Publishing, and he could do it as well here as anywhere else.

But when the fresh coffee was poured, all dark and rich and steamy hot, all Steve saw was the color of Sarah Jordan's eyes. And the cold look of disdain that had been in them.

Chapter Two

"Mark," Steve said, frowning at his uncle with concern and puzzlement. "You do know where your problems are coming from. Right?"

"Sure I do," Mark Donovan said easily. "Poor management—no, make that *lack* of management. For about the last two, two and a half years."

"Okay," Steve said, leaning forward, elbows on knees, fingers loosely clasped. "So what's going on?"

Behind his desk, Mark Donovan sighed, removed his steel-rimmed glasses and polished them with a wrinkled handkerchief. "I've got good people here, Steve-O. I guess you've found that out?"

Steve nodded, and there was an absent wish that his uncle would stop calling him that. But after thirty-five years of it, he doubted it would ever happen.

"They are good," Steve said. "I think I've met and talked to just about everybody here. I haven't done any deep digging yet, but my instincts tell me that you have a very solid staff. That's one of the first things I try to feel out when a company's in trouble. But everyone seems very loyal, hardworking and capable."

"Handpicked." Mark nodded, proud. "I personally do all the hiring and firing. I want to know who I've got on my team." He kept on polishing those specs, looking in Steve's direction with unfocused eyes. "Good people," he said again. "But every ship needs a captain to stay on course."

Steve nodded again. "What happened to the captain, Mark? You're the best."

"I *was* the best." He slipped his glasses back onto the bridge of his nose. His balding pate gleamed blue-green under the fluorescent tubes concealed in the ceiling. "Or at least I was adequate." He smiled, chuckled, then sobered. "And then I guess I just got tired."

"Two years ago," Steve said, beginning to see the big picture. "Did all this start when Aunt Mo died?"

"Mmm," Mark Donovan murmured. "I thought it would pass. I thought it was just one of those humps you have to get over. But, Steve-O? I tell you, it was just never the same. Never will be. I can see that now."

Steve's gaze slid to the opposite side of the room. An empty desk. Maureen's desk. She and Mark had worked together in this office for thirty-five years.

"I understand," Steve said, but knew that he wouldn't *really* understand unless he someday found himself in that same position. For himself, he'd probably still think that work would be the answer to loneliness. After all, it was the answer now, wasn't it?

He was thirty-five years old. Last week he'd found some gray in his hair. If it wasn't for his work, which he loved, his life would be pretty empty. A barren wasteland, his sister Claire called it—and that *included* his work. But Claire had been known to overdramatize.

"I have to tell you something, Steve-O," Mark said, his gaze direct. "A confession of sorts."

"Oh?"

Mark nodded and frowned. "I'm afraid I asked you here under slightly false pretenses."

"Oh?" Now Steve was frowning, too. He had cut time from a heavy schedule to help his uncle. Surely this whole thing wasn't some kind of a lark.

"I'm retiring, Steve-O," Mark said. "Finally ready to hand over the reins. Only trouble is...I don't have anybody to hand them to. Jack's going to stay in construction. Kate has decided to stay home with her kids. And Terry... well, you know Terry. Insurance salesman one week, beach bum the next.''

''I see,'' Steve said cautiously, but he wasn't altogether sure that he did. If his uncle was retiring, why mess with bringing him in when new management would have its own ideas?

Obviously, therein lay the false pretenses, although Steve couldn't see what they were.

''So,'' Steve said. ''You want me to help you scout some talent?''

''The thing is,'' Mark said. ''Houston Publishing has always been a *family* business. My great-great-grandfather on my mother's side started it, and there's always been a Houston or direct descendant as CEO. Until now. I don't like that. I guess that's why it's taken me so long to give it up. But at the same time, I can't just sit here and twiddle my thumbs and let the whole company fall apart.'' He peered at Steve. ''You see my point.''

''Sure,'' Steve said, again cautiously. ''But what—''

''I know. What does all this have to do with why I asked you here?'' Mark leaned back in his ancient swivel chair. Springs and old leather creaked. ''Obviously, we do need some help. Of course, whoever takes over could do their own revitalization. Right? Or at least they should probably have some say in the planning.''

''Right,'' Steve said, finally sure of something.

"Right," Mark echoed. He opened his mouth, hesitated, then plunged right into the thing he'd been pussyfooting around.

"Steve," he said, leaving off the O for the first time, possibly, in history. "I brought you into Chicago to ask if you'd consider taking the job. Will you run Houston Publishing for me, Steve? For all of us? Please don't answer now. Do your job, come up with a brilliant new plan for Houston's, just as we agreed. But while you're doing it, I just ask that you keep the offer in mind. Keep your eyes open enough to see whether Houston's could make you as happy as it's always made me."

It was the last thing Steve had expected Mark to say. Really, the *last* thing. He already *had* a job. A great job. A job that took him all over the world. A job that challenged him to the fullest and compensated him well. A job that kept him so blessedly busy that he didn't have time to think about some of the other things he was lacking. A job that was more than a job, more than a career. A job that had somehow become his life.

So while he was very flattered by Mark's offer and promised to think about it, he knew there was nothing to even consider.

When you depended on something to provide you with everything, you did not give it up.

"Okay, coaches," Patty, the nurse, said. "During the first stage of labor, this is your job. Number one: Be *calm* and have confidence in yourself. Your presence and companionship are the most important contributions. You have a unique tie with the mother...."

At the last statement, Sarah felt Diane's swift glance. *Swift, pitying glance,* she told herself, and raised her chin an inch.

She should never have given in and allowed Diane to come, no matter how much the woman had insisted...and no matter how much Sarah had wanted someone with whom she could share this experience. It simply wasn't Diane's problem, and from the instant they'd walked into the large classroom, Sarah had known she'd made a mistake. Even if time wasn't an issue, as Diane had insisted, there were other things to consider. Like the awkwardness of the whole situation. Sarah felt it, and Diane probably felt it more, on Sarah's behalf.

Thinking about it made her sit straighter—taller. Prouder.

So what if she was the only one in the entire class of thirty who was there with a friend instead of a mate? So what if she knew that everyone there was speculating about her circumstances?

So what if she knew that Diane Fitzgerald practically wanted to weep with pity every time she looked at her.

Diane, happily ensconced in a beautiful home with a wonderful husband and two adorable children, simply could not relate. It was beyond her imagination to understand how Sarah could manage everything on her own.

But of course, Sarah was well accustomed to handling things on her own. Being a single mother was not something she had planned or foreseen, but it *was* something she could handle. After that first shocked week or two, she felt she had adjusted quickly and well. But again, adjusting and managing for herself were things at which she'd had plenty of practice. It would take more than unexpected single motherhood to knock her out of the game.

"All right, everyone," the nurse said, lifting a lemon-yellow folder. "Open your packets and find page one. Follow along, and if there's anything you don't understand, please ask questions."

During the first hour, they went over the different stages of labor and delivery. The handout sheets listed what to expect physically and emotionally, and what to do to make things easier, including the coach's role. The first stage of labor was the longest and progressed over an average of eight to twelve hours from the first mild contraction to full dilation and serious pain. The second stage was pushing and delivery. The third stage, placental separation and expulsion.

When they finished with that, the nurse called for a break.

Sarah pushed up from her folding chair, feeling exhausted just from imagining what she would be going through in seven or eight weeks. Still trying to absorb it all, she headed for the water fountain in the hall outside the classroom.

She drank for a good sixty seconds, holding her hair away from the stream of water. A line formed behind her.

"Not thirsty, were you?" Diane said as they wandered toward the door. It was eight o'clock and the rest of the large doctors' complex was quiet, shut down for the night.

"I'm always thirsty," Sarah said. "And the extra water goes straight to my ankles. It's stuffy in here. Let's go outside."

The September night, muggy and still, held no hint of impending autumn.

Diane stopped next to the glass door, holding her opened information folder so the interior light would fall on it while she read.

"You know," she said, "it's amazing how much of this stuff you forget. I swore that I'd never forget any of it—the pregnancies, the classes, the exercises, the *deliveries*. But you do. I guess that's why people have more than one baby. If they really remembered all the details, they'd probably never do it again."

Sarah laughed. "Probably not. It sounds awful."

"It is," Diane said, serious. "I can't imagine anything worse." Her face softened into a tender smile. "But I can't imagine anything better than what you get in the end, either. It's incredible the way it works, Sarah. While you're in labor, you're sure you must be going to die or something. But the minute you see that tiny little face, that soft, fuzzy little head, those tiny little fingers and toes and...well, nothing else matters. In that instant, you fall in love for the rest of your life."

"I already have," Sarah said, smiling softly, rubbing her swollen belly. "The first time the baby moved...I don't know. It was something."

"Yes," Diane said. "It *is* something."

A silence fell, and for some reason Sarah felt awkward. Too many things unsaid, she thought. Too much pity and worry bottled up inside Diane.

"I shouldn't have given in and had you come with me," Sarah said.

Diane looked up sharply, frowning. "Why not?"

"You're uncomfortable."

"No I'm not—"

"Yes you are. So am I. A little. But it'll get better."

Diane shrugged. "I'm not uncomfortable on my behalf—just yours. I just keep thinking that things shouldn't be this way for you."

"I'm okay, you know," Sarah said.

Diane blinked, as if giving herself a mental shake. "Of course you are." Falsely cheery, probably wanting to hug her and cry.

Diane was such a romantic, always troubled by what should have been and wasn't. Sarah, on the other hand, was a hard-core realist. Not that things didn't get to her from time to time. Especially now, when she felt more physically and emotionally vulnerable than she ever had in her life. Sure, she would have liked to have a loving husband here with her, sharing the experience. Who wouldn't? And sure, she would prefer that her baby come into the world with two devoted parents. But that was not to be, and mourning the impossible was a stupid, senseless waste of time.

"Really, Diane, I'm not so unhappy as you imagine I am. I just wish you'd stop worrying about me all the time and—"

"I'm not worried," Diane said brightly. "Not about you. You're too tough to worry about, kid."

"Liar. I can see it in your eyes every time you look at me. You don't have to feel sorry for me, you know. I don't have it so bad. I'm not destitute. I'm not homeless. I have a career that I love and a beautiful little baby on the way. The only thing I don't happen to have is a husband, and let me tell you, my friend, I can think of a whole lot of worse things to be without. Every woman does not have to have a man to be happy."

"Of course they don't," Diane said. "It's just that Gary was such a—"

"Jerk," Sarah said.

"Right. And the whole thing seems so...unfair. I just hate that this happened to you. I'd like to track him down and—" her soft blue eyes turned murderous "—castrate him."

Sarah laughed, loud and long, and the tension between them fell away.

"Come on," Sarah said, noticing couples filing back into the ocher-carpeted classroom. "It looks like they're getting ready to start again." She grinned at Diane. "How about it, Coach? Are you ready to go stand out in a crowd?"

Diane smiled, but there was a mistiness in her eyes. "Are you kidding?" she said. "I can't wait. I *live* for the opportunity to make a spectacle of myself. Don't you?"

"Apparently," Sarah murmured dryly, and moved aside as Diane headed for the door.

Holding her chin high and proud, Diane pulled the door open and ushered Sarah in ahead of her.

The men had moved all the folding chairs to the sides of the room, clearing the center of the floor.

"Okay," nurse Patty said, all cheery and brisk and ready to get down to business. "Get your pillows and spread out your blankets. Coaches, follow along in your packets. It's exercise time..."

* * *

There was something about the childbirth class that made the baby's arrival seem much more real, as if it really, honestly *was* going to happen. It was hard to imagine, Sarah thought, as she pulled into the parking lot at work the next morning.

It was so hard to imagine that within a few short weeks she would have her very own baby. There would be a new human being on the earth. She grinned at the grand thought that she was doing her part to people the world. Really, that was quite an accomplishment.

She parked the car and reached into the passenger seat to gather up the stacks of work she continually took home. Nights, weekends, sometimes it seemed like those were the only times she ever got any real work done. At the office there were always so many interruptions, so many meetings.

But she did love her work. And that, plus the after-hours time she put in, was another thing Gary had resented, although he'd never seemed to resent cashing her paychecks. But he'd hated the fact that her career took time and energy and attention away from him.

A jazz musician, Gary Ramsay had, in the beginning, been her romantic ideal. Adventurous, funny, daring, talented, outrageous—or so he had seemed at the time. She had met him at a club one Friday night, and four weeks to the day later they had been married. A few weeks after that, and they had been talking about divorce.

All the traits that had so attracted her in the beginning had been nothing but euphemisms. Adventurous and daring were really recklessness to the point of danger and stupidity. From the first day, he'd strained against the boundaries of marriage—a marriage he had pushed for all the way—like a man locked up in a tiny box.

The whole thing had been a horrible mistake, doomed from the start.

Yet when she'd realized that you can't trust birth control, the news of her pregnancy had spawned some hope. Maybe a baby was just what they needed to bring them closer together, settle them down. Instead, of course, the news of the baby had been the final straw.

You're what? Gary had screamed, horror struck. *Sarah, how in the hell could you have been so stupid—*

From outside the car, a lazy male voice intruded on her thoughts.

"Didn't your mother ever tell you that if you frowned too long, your face would stay that way?"

Sarah jumped, startled, and saw Steven Carlisle lounging—he always seemed to be lounging—against the side of a car a couple of empty parking spaces away. From his relaxed stance and the grin on his face, he seemed to have been watching her for some time.

She stiffened and wondered just how much her expressions had revealed. "Good morning, Mr. Carlisle," she said tightly. "I didn't realize you were standing there." There was an implied criticism of his invasion of her privacy, but he either missed it or ignored it, for there was no apology forthcoming.

"Apparently not," he said. "You were off in some other world—a war-torn world, by the looks of you."

Sarah gritted her teeth then forced a bright smile. "Not really. I just tend to frown a lot when I think."

She rummaged through her purse, pretending to be searching for something of vast importance. This was his cue to leave. The conversation was finished. Over. Kaput.

There was a long moment of silence, during which she refused to look at him, but felt him watching her.

"Beautiful day," he said.

"It's hot," Sarah replied. Chicago, even in early September, could get very steamy. Today was going to be a scorcher. Already the heat was building up inside her car.

Prior to her pregnancy, the heat had never bothered Sarah. But now, heat had the same effect on her as the smell of frying bacon or a sizzling charcoal grill—instant queasiness that could quickly turn into violent nausea.

She wished he would leave and looked at him pointedly.

He smiled and stayed right where he was.

"Listen," he said. "I wonder if I could ask a favor."

She raised one eyebrow.

"What kind of favor?"

He shrugged. "Well, Ms. Jordan, it's this way. I'm new to Chicago. Don't have any friends here, other than Mark, of course, but I can only impose on him for so long. Anyway, it can get kind of lonely after a while, you know? And dull, really dull."

Sarah's hands tightened on the steering wheel. She hadn't expected this, but suddenly realized she should have. His asking her out would fit the pattern of his type to a T. She loathed him and all he stood for.

"I would think a man in your position would be too busy *working* to get bored," she said. "According to Mark, Houston Publishing hasn't got a lot of time."

"I'm busy," he said. "But I can't work every minute or my mind overloads. Besides, I still have to eat. That's what I wanted to ask—if you'd consider taking pity on a stranger in town and have lunch with me today."

She started to say no, planning to brush him off with the coldness and polite excuses that everyone uses to fend off unwanted suitors. Then, however, something stopped her.

She stared at him, seeing that easy smile that had charmed so many, no doubt hurt so many, and a slow rage built inside her, urging a confrontation—a full exposure of his character and motives.

"Why me?" she challenged. But she knew. And despised him for it.

A frown pulled his brows together. "What do you mean, why you?"

Sarah's smile was brittle ice, sharp and cutting and colder than cold. After Gary, she knew how to deal with this kind of charmer.

They were all alike, this particular type. Too smooth, too good-looking, too practiced, self-involved, shallow and phoney. The only thing that occasionally threw them was their quarry going on the offense. With honesty—something the Don Juans of the world could not understand.

"I mean, why me?" Her eyes held steady, never leaving his face. "There's a whole building full of drooling females right over there," she said, gesturing toward the large office building. "You know as well as I do that plenty of women are just waiting for you to ask them out. You also know, from our meeting the other day, that I'm not one of those women. So, like I said before, why me?"

She paused, challenging him to deny the truth. He was frowning, thrown by the unexpected attack.

Bravo, Sarah thought, silently applauding herself. *You've come a long way, baby. A year ago, you wouldn't have handled this nearly so well.*

He suddenly grinned and brought his hands up, palms facing the sky in a gesture of bewildered surrender.

"I don't know what to say." And that was an understatement. Sitting there, staring him down, she looked like some dark, dangerous cat poised for the kill. He had the feeling that if he told her the truth, that he had been more attracted to her on sight than to any other woman in recent remembrance, she'd pounce on him and tear him to pieces.

"Why don't you try the truth?" she said, challenge obvious in everything about her. Her face was rigid. Her dark, dark eyes were flashing danger signals. And her husky-velvet voice barely smoothed a knife edge.

What the hell was going on here? Steve thought. Why did *she* think he'd asked her out? It wasn't as if she was the boss's daughter or he was some hopeful writer out to romance her into publishing his work. As far as he knew, there was nothing for him to gain by dating her...nothing, at least, related to business.

"All right," he said, eyes narrowing with sudden decision. "The *truth*, Ms. Jordan, is that I asked you because I was more attracted to you than anyone else."

He wouldn't have thought it possible for her face to look any harder, but it did. Then she did something he would have never expected. She laughed, a harsh sound without pleasure or amusement.

"You're priceless, Carlisle," she said, shaking her head. "Anyway, the answer is no. No, I don't want to have lunch with you. But thank you so much for asking, just the same." She turned away and began gathering her belongings from the seat beside her.

After her reactions, which Steve thought inappropriate and uncalled for, he had no intention of being so easily dismissed.

"I take it, Ms. Jordan, that you don't believe that what I told you was the truth."

She spared him a scathing glance. "Not by a long shot, buster. Now, if you'll excuse me, I've got to get to work." He watched her run a brush through her straight, glossy hair, then fluff back her feathery bangs with her fingertips.

"Okay, Ms. Jordan, I'll bite. Why do *you* think I invited you to lunch?"

Her head whipped around, her gaze piercing. Yet, beneath the hard anger he thought he glimpsed something else. Sadness?

"I'm not playing games here," she said in a lower voice than before. "I know why. You know why. The only *possible* reason in the world is that I present a challenge. I'm probably the only single woman in the building who you knew would turn you down, and your ego couldn't stand the knowledge that I wasn't interested in you. It's all a game, and you can't stand to lose. I think that's revolting.''

"So do I," Steve said, stunned at what she'd come up with. Why didn't she believe the truth? Couldn't she see in the mirror? She was gorgeous, but apparently her self-image was so low that the concept of his attraction to her was inconceivable in her mind.

Whatever anger he'd felt at her treatment of him went away. This woman had been hurt. Oh, yes, she was angry inside, but it was an anger born of pain. Why else would she feel that she was so undesirable, unless she had been beaten down by someone or something along the way.

"That's not the reason," he said gently, wanting to persuade. "The minute we met, I felt a sort of...I don't know, chemistry, I guess."

"Mmm." Sarah nodded, heavy sarcasm screaming from her thoughtful expression. "Well, I guess I can understand that. I mean, not many men would be able to resist this gorgeous body, would they? Right about now, I must have sex symbol written all over me."

Steve shook his head. "Sarah, I don't understand what this—"

"Give me a break," she said, rolling her eyes. She suddenly sounded very tired of the whole thing.

"Now, enjoyable as it's been, I'm afraid I'm going to have to cut this little tête-à-tète short. Some of us around here have a lot of work to do."

She rolled up the car window and opened the door.

Chapter Three

He was frowning, trying to think of what to say to change her opinion of him, when she swung her legs out of the car and stood up.

At that moment, his mind went blank.

She stood there in profile, and his mouth dropped open in shock.

This couldn't be.

No.

This was impossible.

He blinked, rubbed a hand over his mouth, then held it there. And stared.

Sarah looked at him and scowled. "Knock it off, will you, Carlisle?"

He dragged his gaze away from that mound of a stomach, and in a daze, met her eyes. "Huh?" he said, finally dropping his hand from his mouth. "What did you say?"

"I said, knock it off." Irritated, she slammed the car door.

"Knock what off?" he asked, and looked at her belly one more time. It was like a magnet, drawing him back and back, taunting him with the blatant evidence of his own incredible idiocy.

This was a joke, right?

She was going to play a joke on someone at the office and had stuffed a pillow—or six—under that tent of a dress.

Because nobody, *nobody*, could be so stupid as to not notice that this woman was very pregnant.

Her left arm was loaded down with half a dozen fat manila file folders. Her huge natural-straw handbag hung from its strap on her right shoulder. She put her free hand on her hip.

"I know what you're doing," she said. "You're standing there trying to think how you can prove that I'm wrong about you. Well forget it, because even if I were wrong about you, I'm still not interested."

Her words, reminding him of their conversation, snapped him out of his daze.

"I know," he said, and swiftly crossed the fifteen feet of asphalt that separated them. His mind racing, he took her arm.

"I know," he said again, and licked his lips. He felt nearly frantic to make her understand. The idea of trying to romance this woman now seemed... reprehensible, nearly obscene. It was imperative that she know that about him. "I understand now," he said. "I'm sorry. If I had known, I would never have...I mean..." He stopped, ran his hand through his hair, aware that he was floundering. He took a quick, deep breath. "I'm really very sorry. I just didn't know."

She was frowning, alarmed and none too pleased about the way he was lunging at her and babbling.

"Didn't know what?" she snapped, yanking her arm away from him.

He backed off immediately, giving her some space. "About—" he gestured toward her belly "—about...the baby."

"What about it?" Her frown deepened and her hand moved automatically to her stomach. "What are you talking about?"

He was handling this badly. It had just come as such a shock.

"Look," he said. "I didn't know you were pregnant. If I had—"

Sarah stared. "What do you mean you didn't know I was pregnant? How could you *not* know? Good heavens, Carlisle, how could *anyone* not know?"

That was a perfectly good question. Steve wracked his brain to recall the times he'd seen her. There had only been two. That first time, in her office. And this morning, in her car.

"I don't know," he said. "I guess you were always hidden, at least the bottom half of you. When we met, you were behind your desk the whole time, and all that junk on top... and today, you were in your car... I don't know. I feel like the world's biggest ass."

And he looked as if he felt that way, too, Sarah thought, believing the contrition in his face. He looked absolutely miserable.

She stood there for a minute, relishing it. And letting it all sink in.

If Steven Carlisle had known she was pregnant, he would never have tried to romance her, never have been attracted to her at all.

She believed that. He looked too positively miserable to be lying.

Which changed things quite a bit.

She still didn't like his general type, but at least he was showing that he did possess a small streak of decency, something that, five minutes ago, she'd been sure that he, like Gary, existed completely and happily without.

A man who considered *any* woman fair game? No, Sarah thought, with a small smile. Not any woman. Not her. Judging by the look on his face, she wouldn't be able to interest him romantically even if she threw herself at him.

And that suited Sarah just fine.

"Mr. Carlisle..." she began, feeling benevolent, and, as the humor of the situation began to sink in, she had to stifle a chuckle. "It's quite obvious that there have been a few...misconceptions on both our sides." She had to stop for a second to compose a straight face. Really, the whole thing was inordinately funny.

She kept seeing his expression as he'd rushed up to apologize to her—and the mortification when he'd tried to explain.

Suddenly she burst out laughing.

And it felt so good, was such a release of so much tension, she just kept on laughing.

He looked at her reproachfully. "It's really not that funny."

"It's pretty funny," she insisted, eyes watering from laughing so hard.

"Go ahead and gloat," he said. "I'll bet nobody ever accused you of being a good sport."

Which only made her laugh harder. She slipped one hand under her weighty stomach to support it.

Finally, she brought herself under control.

He watched her with narrowed green eyes. "Done?" he asked.

"Done." She nodded and had to struggle not to start again. For the first time in a long time, she felt really, really good and had laughed until she'd cried. Maybe there was something to the old line about laughter being the best medicine.

"I'm sorry," she said, wiping her eyes. "I didn't mean to gloat."

"You should be sorry," he said, then his mouth slanted wryly. "I suppose, though, that under the absurd circumstances, I had it coming."

"I suppose I may have overreacted earlier," she conceded graciously. "Lately I am a little overly sensitive."

His gaze went once more to her stomach. He stared for a minute, then shook his head, as if still not believing what he saw. Or how he could have missed it in the beginning.

When he returned his gaze to her face, there was a warm sparkle of humor in his eyes that was not the least sexual or flirty, just sort of humble and... candid. Sarah liked it.

"Ms. Jordan, I'd like to make a proposal. Let's start over, shall we? I mean *all* over—completely. I don't know about you, but I'd really like to pretend that these first two meetings never existed."

"All right," Sarah said, fighting a grin. "Let's start over."

He held out a hand. "Hi. My name's Steve Carlisle. I'm the hotshot Mark brought in to *really* screw things up. In the business, they call me Sherlock, because I never miss a trick. The tiniest detail can't escape my finely honed observational powers—''

She was laughing again, holding the aching muscles along the sides of her stomach. "Stop, stop!" she begged. "Enough! Unless you want to help me have this baby right in the middle of the parking lot!"

It was a joke, but the effect on Steve was instantaneous—and sobering.

"Let's go," he said, and took her by the elbow, propelling her quickly but carefully toward the building.

This time, Sarah did not snatch her arm away.

"You're kidding," Diane Fitzgerald said, eyes huge with disbelief.

"I'm not." Sarah grinned. Her bare feet were propped on cartons of manuscripts, hands resting atop her belly.

"He really didn't *know*? That is so incredible! Oh, Sarah, I bet he about died, didn't he?"

"Just about. Suffice it to say it was a…humbling experience."

They sat for a moment, letting the scene play again in their imaginations. In the same instant, they burst out laughing.

There was a knock at her office door.

"Entrez!" Sarah called gaily.

The laughter collapsed into guilty silence as Steve appeared in the doorway.

"Steve," Sarah said, avoiding his eyes. "Come in. What can I do for you?"

He looked at Diane, then back at Sarah. "I seem to be interrupting," he said, looking distinctly uncomfortable. One hand tugged at his collar. The other was behind his back. "I'll check back with you later."

"No," Diane said, jumping to her feet. "You stay. Really. I was just leaving."

"No, no," he insisted, backing away. "I've got to get to a meeting anyway." He looked at Sarah. "Later, Sarah. It wasn't important."

He pulled the door closed as he left.

With raised eyebrows, Sarah looked at Diane.

"I wonder what he wanted," Diane said. "Obviously it was something private. When he saw me, he couldn't get out of here fast enough."

Sarah sobered and took her feet down. It was time to get back to work.

"I hope, Diane, that Golden Boy Carlisle was here to talk about business. Somebody had better do something around here to save this company or there isn't going to be one to worry about." She put her empty yogurt container in the trash and her lunch thermos in her desk drawer.

Glancing at her watch, Diane headed for the door. "Don't worry about Houston's, Sarah. I have a gut feeling that everything is going to be just fine. Really. Just have faith.''

"I'm trying," Sarah said grimly. "But I'll feel a whole lot better when and if we start seeing some progress around here." It was so important that Houston's pull through this mess. Important for Mark, of course, and for her because she cared about him.

But important, too, for herself and her baby. She had been with the company nearly seven years. Mark knew her, trusted her, respected her. Which was why, when she had gone to Mark with her proposal a few months ago, he had listened with an open mind and been generous in his willingness to work with her on it.

At Houston Publishing, her future was well planned and worry free.

But if she had to go somewhere else? Sarah didn't have to be told that she'd be starting all over. No one else would even consider her plans.

And that would ruin everything she'd worked so hard to build.

Come on, Carlisle, she thought, biting her lip. *Shock me, stun me, prove me wrong just one more time. And manage to do something wonderful for Houston Publishing.*

The flowers arrived just before quitting time. Sarah had been out of her office, attending a meeting. She stopped short, just inside the door, and stared at the small but lavish bouquet on her desk.

Pink, powder blue, white, yellow, lavender, mint green, aqua....

The pastel flowers were the tiny kind. Miniature roses and carnations, baby's breath and a few flowers Sarah couldn't name.

The container was a white porcelain baby shoe. The card read:

Sorry I missed you, but maybe, under the circumstances, that was for the best. Since I've heard that an upset mother can mean an upset baby, the flowers are an apology to both of you.
Sincerely,
Steve

Oh, and P.S. Since we don't know yet whether we need pink or blue, I asked the florist to include any and all flowers that might possibly be appropriate. Personally, I think she got a little carried away.

Personally, Sarah thought the extravagantly colored arrangement was beautiful. And the white porcelain shoe was so—

Abruptly, she straightened her shoulders and pulled the misty smile from her lips.

Apologies were fine, and now he had made more than were necessary. She would write a brief, gracious note of thanks and leave it at that.

She didn't want flowers from him or apologies or anything else.

All she wanted from Steven Carlisle was results. And she just couldn't shake the sinking feeling that she was hoping for entirely too much.

"Okay, everybody, that's it," nurse Patty said. "Practice your exercises, and we'll see you next time."

Lying on the floor, Sarah struggled to sit up and wondered aloud why all the other pregnant women seemed to manage this task more easily than she did.

"They don't," Diane said, helping to hoist her to her feet. "It just seems like it. And probably everyone here is thinking the same thing."

Sarah was dubious. She adjusted the striped tent of a rugby shirt she was wearing and waddled toward the door. Every day she felt bigger and bigger.

"It's because the baby's dropping," Diane had told her earlier. "It stretches you where you hadn't been stretched before."

Lovely. Now she could have matching stretch marks on several parts of her body.

"Gripe, gripe, gripe," Diane had told her more than once that day. "Since when are you so negative about everything?"

She was just in a rotten mood, that was the problem. Had been for the last several days. The pressure was getting to her.

There was so much work to do before the baby came, both at the office and around the apartment. The baby was due in six weeks and Sarah didn't even have the nursery ready.

The crib was still in the box, unassembled. The walls were an ugly green color that was totally unsuitable. There were no toys arranged on shelves, no wall decorations. Nothing but a tiny, drab room full of junk.

And the office... just thinking about it all made her head begin to pound. Time was going so fast. In the beginning, nine months had seemed like an eternity. Now, already, the end was almost here.

"You okay?" Diane asked, noticing Sarah's expression with concern.

"Sure." Sarah stopped at her car. "Just tired. You know."

"I know. Listen, Sarah, why don't I come back to the apartment with you and we'll order a pizza or something and kick back for an hour or two and just relax. No work, no problems, just a good long gab session and some good, fattening food."

Sarah shook her head wearily. "Sounds tempting, but I can't. Really. I just have too much to do."

"An hour or two won't make any difference."

"Honestly, I can't. I—"

"Come on, Sarah. Indulge yourself a little. Indulge me. You deserve a break, kiddo. Take it."

Sarah bit her lip, then gave in. "Okay. Let's do it. And I'll try not to feel guilty until tomorrow."

"Sarah, this place is a *wreck*!" Diane's eyes were wide with dismay as she looked around the so-called nursery. All the baby's stuff was in there all right, but it was all in bags and boxes and mixed in with tools and dropcloths and waiting cans of paint.

Mouth tightening, Diane turned to face Sarah. "I asked you weeks ago—*months* ago—how the nursery was coming along and if you needed any help. You said fine, and no, you did not want help. Sarah, this is not, by *any* stretch of the imagination, fine!"

"I know," Sarah said, rolling her head from side to side to ease the tension in her neck. "And I *don't* need any help. I'm going to get to it soon. But first I've got to get ahead of things at work, just in case the baby should decide to come early. I have to have everything ready so Laura can step in without any trouble."

"Laura is not an idiot." Diane scowled. "She's been working with you for three years! Trust me, Sarah, she can handle the magazine while you're gone."

"I just don't want any problems," Sarah said evenly, but this was a subject she felt very strongly about. The magazine was more than just a job. It was her baby, too. She had nurtured it and helped it grow. She loved it. And always looming over her head was the possibility that she might lose it.

She let out a long, tense sigh and rubbed a hand over her forehead and eyes. "Diane, what am I going to do if Houston's folds?"

There was a long moment of silence. Then Diane put a comforting arm around her shoulders and steered her away from the depressing sight of the ugly, green room and into the small, cluttered living room.

"If that should happen," Diane said, urging Sarah into the old corduroy recliner and propping her swollen feet on the footrest. "And I do mean *if*, because I don't believe it will. But if it should, we'll do whatever we have to do to work things out. *We*, Sarah. You're not in this all alone, much as you'd like to be." A wry smile slanted Diane's mouth. "Friends help each other—and lean on each other when they need to. That's a fact of life you somehow missed along the way, but you might as well get used to the idea."

Sarah closed her eyes, feeling close to exhaustion. "I had it all worked out," she murmured. "Everything was going to be perfect."

After the baby was born, she had Mark's approval to stay home and work out of the house, except for the couple of mornings a week on which she'd go to the office for meetings and anything she couldn't handle from home.

She opened her eyes. "It was going to be ideal, Diane. I could be home with my baby and still run the magazine. And now..."

"And now," Diane said firmly. "Nothing has changed. Yet."

"I know," Sarah grumbled. "That's the problem. Golden Boy has been here, what—two weeks? And nothing has changed. I think that's what's getting to me most of all. I'm working my fanny off for the future, and all the time I'm worrying that there isn't going to be one—at least not there. It makes it twice as hard."

"Okay," Diane said briskly, holding up a hand to stop the flow of negativity. "Enough. Worrying about it isn't going to change anything. So I suggest we start worrying about something we can change— like that pitiful excuse for a nursery. I'm going to go take a look and see where we should start."

"No," Sarah said, dropping the footrest and starting to get up. "I can do it myself. I'm planning to start on it next week. But first I need to—"

Diane stopped and turned around. "*First*, you need to sit back down and put those feet up before your ankles explode. And second, you need to get your priorities in order. A job is just a job. If you have to, you can find another. And Laura can fill in for you without any trouble. But this baby...just think about it, Sarah! I mean, really *think* about it. You're going to have a *brand-new baby* in this house!''

A *brand-new baby*!

A brand-new baby in a few short weeks and nothing was ready!

Diane was right. What *had* she been thinking of?

Over the weekend, Sarah took time to make an inventory of what she had and what she still needed to get. Since she was new at all this, she culled her lists of needs from magazines and Diane. There were a lot of things that never would have occurred to her.

Like diapers. Since she planned to use the disposables, it had never entered her mind that she'd need at least a dozen of the cloth ones, too. *Burp cloths,* Diane had said, nodding sagely. *The first rule of thumb. Don't ever put a new baby up on your shoulder without some protection.*

And formula, for just in case. Since she planned to nurse, Sarah had never thought about having some canned formula on hand in case of emergency—or for a very large appetite.

And a diaper bag. Very obvious to probably anyone else, but somehow Sarah had completely overlooked the fact that when you take a baby somewhere, you take a whole load of supplies along with you.

And the list went on and on.

For the last several months, she'd been picking up things here and there. Baby lotions, baby powders, baby oils—all of which, of course, Diane told her she didn't even really need. She'd bought neutral-colored—white, yellow—sleep sacques and a few soft, tiny blankets, but not much else in the way of clothing. She'd wait on that until the baby was born and then get things that were meant for a definite girl or boy.

Girl. Or boy. That was another thing. It seemed incredible that a new little person was coming and she had no instinctive inkling of what gender it would be. Which didn't seem right. After all, she was the mother. It just sort of seemed like she should know.

The doctor's guess, based on the baby's fast heart rate, was a boy.

The woman at Scharp's delicatessen down the block, based on the way Sarah was carrying the baby, predicted a girl.

And Sarah, of course, didn't know.

By the time she got to work Monday morning, she felt better than she had the previous week. The hours spent not thinking about Houston's and its problems had been like therapy, smoothing out some of the tensions that had been building for the last several weeks. She felt more rested, more energetic. And finally had her priorities more in order.

When she got home that night, she was not going to work on *Midwest Woman*. She was going to paint the nursery.

By midafternoon the rumors were flying.

There was a new excitement in the air, an energy and enthusiasm that hadn't been there for quite some time. Every time she picked up her phone or went to the washroom or went to the small cafeteria, all Sarah heard was the name Steven Carlisle.

After two weeks of appearing to do nothing, he suddenly turned Houston Publishing upside down.

All day he had scheduled meeting after meeting, with department after department. Art. Editorial. Fiction. Nonfiction. Advertising. Accounting. Marketing. He was briefly laying out plans and ideas and new goals. New, exciting goals, judging by the sparkles in everybody's eyes.

Diane was thrilled. "He's brilliant, Sarah!" she said, bringing a cup of coffee into Sarah's office. "He's going to revolutionize the art department."

"Revolutionize?" Sarah said skeptically. "Come on, there can't be that much to change."

Yet there was, and Diane went into great and enthusiastic detail.

"Sounds good," Sarah had to admit. "But is all that practical? I mean, some of the changes sound expensive and—"

"Oh, good grief, Sarah, will you just admit that you were wrong and that the man actually knows what he's doing? He knows where to spend money and where to cut back. That's his job, remember?" She sipped her coffee, then smiled smugly. "Besides, the accounting department seems happy, too. I couldn't get old Wally to give any details, but he was whistling when he walked down the hall this morning. What does that tell you?"

Sarah raised her eyebrows. "Wally? Whistling? I guess I have to consider that proof positive, don't I?" She pretended reluctance, but the inner weight she'd felt was growing cautiously lighter.

Chapter Four

He poured himself into his work, immersing his mind, body and emotions.

This was not a new experience. When he had a job to do, he gave it his all.

There were different phases involved in a project. The first—preliminary study and research done before he arrived on site. The second—just knocking about, absorbing the atmosphere, meeting the staff, listening to his instincts…giving it all a little time to gel.

Then came the planning, the intensive thinking and brainstorming, the most creative and exciting part of the deal.

After that was the delivery and explanation of ideas to key people, and finally the revisions and the beginning of execution. Normally, the final phase didn't keep him around too long. Good executives didn't need him to put the plans in progress.

Which meant, as far as Houston Publishing was concerned, Steve was almost done. A week, two at most, and he'd be on his way. Back to New York. Then off to Minneapolis, which was next on his crowded agenda.

He chewed on the inside of his cheek and tilted back in his desk chair. He stared at the acoustical-tiled ceiling, hands folded loosely on his stomach.

It was 4:00 p.m.

He had a meeting scheduled. Now.

It was the last of a two-day series of meetings with the department heads of Houston Publishing. The last, not because it was most important or least important or on any particular schedule or agenda. It was the last simply because he'd kept putting it off. It was with Sarah, regarding *Midwest Woman*.

He closed his eyes, rocked farther back in the chair.

Then he got up, because he couldn't find any good reasons to put it off any longer.

The suspense.

It was driving her crazy.

As far as she'd been able to ascertain, Steven Carlisle had met with *everyone* at H.P. except her. Everyone else had come first. And now, to top it all off, he was late.

Sarah's stomach was churning.

She stuffed another saltine cracker—the only medicine allowed for nausea—in her mouth and chewed mechanically. She had really come to loathe saltines.

It was 4:07. He was supposed to have been there at four o'clock.

Was this whole waiting game deliberate? Was he delaying because he still felt awkward and wanted to avoid her? Or perhaps he had bad news about her magazine and didn't want to tell her.

The magazine was small, local, serving just Chicago and the surrounding area. Barely four years old, *Midwest Woman* was not a huge money-maker, but it was never intended to be. It was a new, minor and experimental project for Houston Publishing, which handled mostly technical and textbooks, but dabbled in several other kinds of books on the side, thanks to Mark Donovan's desire and willingness to explore and grow.

He was a man open to possibilities...but was that what had gotten the company into trouble? Would Steve advise that the minimal money-making projects be cut?

Sarah frowned and crunched another saltine.

Someone rapped on her door and she jumped, brushing crumbs from her hands, her mouth, her table of a belly.

She was lowering her feet from the stack of cartons when he walked in, carrying a thick sheaf of papers.

"You're late," she said, adopting the briskness that always came to her when she was nervous or uncomfortable. In both her personal life and in her line of work, she'd learned that you had to get tough—or get trampled.

"I'm sorry," he said, and flashed a brief smile that didn't seem to reach his eyes.

Sarah swallowed and got a saltine from her left-hand desk drawer.

"Excuse me," she said, when he looked at the cracker. "These are for nausea. I can't take medication."

He raised his brows. "You're not feeling well? Listen, let's just postpone this meeting until a better time. I—"

"No," she said, too sharply, then managed to smile. "I mean, I haven't actually felt *well* for the last seven months, so this isn't new to me. I'd really prefer to just get on with it."

He frowned and tipped his head to the side. "I thought pregnant women were only nauseous for the first two or three months—and mostly in the morning."

"That's a crock," Sarah said. "Or at least as far as my experience goes. But anyway, let's talk about something more interesting, shall we?"

"Like business," he said.

"Yes. Like business."

He pulled a chair close to the opposite side of her desk and opened a folder, quickly scanning the contents.

The suspense was killing her.

Sarah wanted to scream. Instead, she reached for another saltine.

"So what I'm suggesting," Steve said, "is expansion."

Sarah blinked, afraid to believe she'd heard him correctly. "Expansion?" Her voice sounded calm, but her heart was pounding.

"*Major* expansion." He grinned. "Right now, *Midwest Woman* is limited to Chicago and the immediate surrounding areas. What I'd like to see you do is expand and broaden it to serve the whole Midwest."

"Oh," she said. "I see."

But her mind was whirling, trying to adjust. This was far more than she had dared to hope for, especially right now, with the company in a money crunch.

From time to time she had daydreamed about expanding the magazine's market and circulation, but

MW had been designed to be a local publication, and she had assumed that was the way it would stay.

But this...this was one of those fabled dreams come true, something very akin to a miracle.

Something, she thought suddenly, *that had to be too good to be true.*

She lowered her eyes, unwilling to let him see her disappointment.

When she looked up, she eyed him levelly, noting again that handsome, boyish-yet-rugged face, those extraordinary pale green eyes. No wonder the place had been buzzing with excitement. No doubt Steve had made his rounds, held his meetings—and told every single person exactly what he wanted to hear.

It all sounded great. It was just too damned bad it couldn't possibly work.

She had been right all along; Golden Boy didn't know what he was doing.

"That all sounds lovely, Steve," she said.

He frowned slightly. "That's it?" he asked. "'It all sounds lovely'?"

She shrugged. "It does. What else did you want me to say?"

He tilted his head, puzzled. "I thought you cared about this magazine."

"I do. Very much."

"But you're not the least bit excited about branching out with it. Why? Are you opposed to growth, Sarah?"

"No," she said. Her eyes grew cold. "Not when it's based on reality."

He had been leaning forward, forearms on her desk. Now he dropped back against his chair and stroked his upper lip with a forefinger.

"Here we go again," he murmured. "Talking in riddles."

Sarah resented that, the implication of playing games. She also resented the way he'd been getting everyone's hopes up when what he proposed surely had to be nothing but fantasy.

"No riddles, Steve. I'm simply saying that I find your proposal for my magazine hard to believe."

"And why, Sarah, is that?" A note of sarcasm had crept into his voice.

Suddenly impatient, she waved a hand through the air. "The money, Carlisle, the money! Do you know what it would cost to do what you're suggesting?"

"More or less," he murmured, but he knew almost to the penny.

He was angered by her quick dismissal of a plan that should have delighted her. And angered, mostly, by her obvious lack of belief in his competence as a professional. There was a natural, immediate urge to jump in, quote figures, prove himself. Yet pride held him back.

Maybe he'd just sit here and let her talk. She was so cynical, so skeptical, so quick to jump to conclusions and condemn.

"More or less?" she repeated, and shook her dark head. "Trust me here, Carlisle, it's *more*. And the way I understand it, Mark's problem with the company is money—*less* money than he's got." She sighed. "Maybe I'm just being real dense here, but would you mind explaining to me just how those two facts are going to add up?"

"Actually, I would," he said, coming to a sudden decision. He leaned forward, swept up the papers from her desk and got to his feet. "I would *mind*, that is. It's late. I don't have time for a lengthy explanation of my overall plans for Houston Publishing—besides, departments other than yours aren't really any of your concern." He tossed the file onto her desk. "Here are the ideas for *Midwest Woman*. Go over them. If you have any questions, you can call me in the morning."

That said, he left.

Stunned, Sarah stared after him for a good long time.

"I'm sorry," she said, the instant he picked up the phone the next morning. "I was insulting and unprofessional—and wrong. Your proposal is very complete and impressive."

He cradled the phone between ear and shoulder and kicked back in his chair, his mouth slanting with a dry kind of satisfaction.

"Ms. Jordan, I presume?"

"Yes. I hope you accept my apology."

He put his feet up on his desk, crossing his legs at the ankles. "Of course," he said.

He could have gone on, making this easier for her. Instead, he let the silence lengthen. She had done nothing but doubt him and judge him since he'd arrived. On the personal level, that was one thing. On the professional level, it was quite another.

He heard her draw a deep breath and wondered what was coming.

"Steve . . . I'm ashamed to have to admit that I've found myself guilty of stereotyping you, hence the way I've acted. When I read your report and saw all the work you'd done, I have to admit I was . . ."

"Shocked? Amazed?"

". . . Yes."

"Why?" He narrowed his eyes and gazed at the ceiling. But he was seeing her, no doubt more vulnerable now than any time he had seen her in person. He had a sudden, stabbing desire to have this conversation face-to-face, to finally behold some softness in those proud, strong features.

"I don't know," she said quietly. "I guess, as I said, I had just cast you into a mold right at the beginning. I don't normally do that kind of thing."

"What kind of mold?" Why didn't he just let it go? he wondered, getting angry with himself. She had apologized, so why not be graceful about it?

Because she's talking to you, a little voice said. *For the first time, she's actually talking to you. Honestly.*

But with that recognition came moral obligation. To continue with this was taking unfair advantage.

"Never mind," he said, before she could answer. "Apology accepted. No hard feelings."

He heard her soft breath of relief that he was letting her off the hook.

"Great," she said, her customary briskness returning already. The sound of papers being shuffled came over the phone lines. "Now, you said that if I had any questions, I should call. I do have a couple of things. Is this a good time?"

He looked at his watch and scowled. "Actually, Sarah, I'm afraid it isn't. I had just stopped in here to pick up some paperwork. I've got a meeting with Mark right about now."

"Oh."

She sounded disappointed, and Steve smiled, liking that. So she *had* gotten excited about his plans, after all. He'd known she would. To anyone in her position, it would be like the world's greatest Christmas present. And lucky him, he frequently got to play Santa Claus, one of the better perks of his job.

"Well," she said. "Maybe we could set up a meeting for some time today. You say when, Steve. I'll rearrange my schedule to suit."

He raised his eyebrows at her willingness to oblige and reached for his appointment book. A frown formed, then deepened as he realized he was booked solid for the next several days. Conscious that she was waiting, he searched for meetings that were unimportant or easily postponed...then, realizing what he was doing, he cursed himself.

What was the matter with him? She had blown the meeting they'd had. Why was he scampering to accommodate her now?

He chewed on his cheek, knowing the answer and not liking it one bit. The fact of the matter was that her pregnancy hadn't altered the pull of attraction he'd felt for her right from the start. Well, maybe it had *altered* it, changed it a bit to accommodate the circumstances. But it had not lessened the attraction at all.

He'd found that out when he'd finally forced himself to go to her office yesterday afternoon. He'd known there was a reason he kept putting her off, but hadn't wanted to examine or acknowledge what that reason might be. And the instant he'd seen her again, it had started all over.

Despicable, that's what it was. Because a decent, honorable man just *didn't* lust after a very pregnant, very vulnerable, very *uninterested* woman. A decent, honorable man left her alone—even in his thoughts. And his hormones.

"I'm sorry," he said, his voice crisp with renewed determination. "I don't have any time available for the next few days. Why don't you get back to me early next week. Things should ease up by then." And maybe by then he'd have taught his traitor body and emotions to make more sense and to have more control. Besides, shortly after that, he'd be leaving.

"Oh," she said, and sighed her disappointed acceptance. "All right. If that's the way it has to be...."

No, he thought. *It can be any way you want it to be....* "I'm sorry," he said again, muscles flexing in his jaw. Then his gaze fastened on an empty slot in his appointment book and wouldn't let go. Temptation lay before him, and all his noble intentions were shot.

"Actually," he said, falsely casual. "I do have about an hour today, but I doubt that you'd want to—"

"An hour would be terrific," she said. "You name the time and place and I'll be there. To tell you the truth, Steve, I'm so excited about this thing, I can hardly stand it."

He smiled and shook his head, rather hating himself for what he was about to do...and the way he was looking forward to doing it.

"The hour I can spare is for lunch, Sarah. I hate to mention it because I've had some experience in how you react to suggestions like that."

There was a brief, heavy pause. At the end of it, she decided to laugh. "Things have changed since then," she said. "This lunch date will be a whole lot different from the first one we both had in mind."

Only for you, Steve thought, and rubbed a hand over his eyes. *I'll still be having lunch with the woman I'm more attracted to than anyone I've met in a long, long time.*

Despicable, he thought again as he hung up the phone.

But the knowledge of the need for self-condemnation only slightly dampened his anticipation. Right or wrong, he was buoyed by it and rode high on it through the rest of the morning.

He drove and was very conscious of her presence in his rented Buick sedan.

He kept stealing quick looks at her and was captivated by the new animation in her face, the new softness and lack of wariness. The new, fairly dazzling smiles on her lips and in her eyes.

She was talking freely and easily, mostly praising and approving and applauding the brilliance of his proposal.

Steve listened and swallowed a lot because his throat kept going dry. He had the sinking *stinking* feeling that this outing was a grave mistake. He was fast becoming more than strongly attracted to this woman.

With each minute that passed, each smile she sent his way, each praising and newly respectful comment, he was leaving the stage of mere attraction and stumbling and bumbling down the road to being well and truly smitten. To caring rather than just feeling. To wanting to share rather than being satisfied with enjoyable, mutual superficiality. To wanting to become involved with Sarah Jordan and her life.

Impossible.

Ridiculous.

But blast it all, he could *feel* it happening.

"Oh," she said, pointing to an upcoming intersection. "Turn right here. I mean—" she laughed "—turn *left* right here."

He gave her a grin and turned the car, then followed her directions to the restaurant. He drove carefully, ultraconscious of her physical vulnerability. And when he had parked, he found himself rushing around to help her out and keeping a protective, guiding grip on her elbow to steer her through the perils of the parking lot and inside to safety.

He had six sisters, and five of them had been pregnant enough times to provide him with a gaggle of nineteen nieces and nephews. And while he had helped the various expectant mothers and was sure he'd been considerate and thoughtful, he could not remember feeling as if he needed to protect them and coddle them like a case of nitro glycerine!

So what was the matter with him now?

"I love it," Sarah said when they had gone over the final page of his prospectus. They had finished lunch and were having coffee—one of the two cups she allowed herself per day. "It's perfect—and workable. You've thought of everything."

"Not everything," he said with the charming modesty Sarah had heard about—and now believed. "That's just an outline, a plan. There are a million details that'll be left up to you."

"I can handle it."

She grinned, relishing the challenge that lay ahead. He was right; there was a huge amount of work to be done in order to make this thing fly. But it was worth it. Oh, was it worth it. She glanced at her notebook, searching the pages of scribbled notes and questions for anything that remained unanswered.

"Oh," she said. "I almost forgot. You had made some notes in one of the margins that I didn't understand. Let's see..." She found the page and handed it across the table to him. "It looks like 'new year, new mag.' What does all that mean?"

He frowned, then relaxed, his mouth sliding into a half grin. "Oh. That was just a half-baked idea for a promotion you could do." He leaned back against the black vinyl booth, waving a hand. "It was just a thought. I'm not sure it was even a very good one, and considering the time involved, I don't think it's workable anyway. Let's forget it. Are you sure you don't want any dessert?''

"No," Sarah said. "I mean, no thanks on the dessert, and no, let's not just forget about your idea. Tell me."

She had learned hard and well that he had a good mind under all that charm and physical attractiveness. If he had an idea, workable or not, she wanted to hear it.

He shrugged and toyed with the handle of his coffee cup. "It really wasn't that big a deal," he said. "It just struck me that with a new year coming up real soon, you might be able to capitalize on it to launch your magazine."

"How so?" Sarah said, eyes narrowing in thought.

"By launching it in January. A new year is something people always get a little excited about."

"So," Sarah said, catching on. "We promote both to gain more attention. A new year, a new magazine."

"I also thought you might make a few format changes, as well. You know, a little more high-tech, just to support the whole 'new' concept." He paused, then shrugged again. "But like I said, it's half baked. Marketing and promotion are not exactly my lines."

"It's terrific!" Sarah said, and meant it. "I love it."

"Yeah?" Steve grinned, and something warm glittered in his eyes.

"Yeah." Sarah bobbed her head. "I think we should go with it."

His grin faded. "There's a catch. You'd have to be ready to roll with everything by January."

Sarah's grin faded, too. It was mid-September now. And the baby was due in a little over a month. Under the best of circumstances, it would be a major undertaking. Under her circumstances, she didn't know if it was at all possible or not. Still, the opportunity seemed too good to miss.

"I can do it," she said, chin lifting with resolve. "Or die trying."

And before he could stop them, three fateful and ridiculous words slipped out of Steve's mouth.

"I could help," he said. And knew he was lost.

Chapter Five

Y ou can't do that!" Thelma Grant said, from Steve's office in New York.

"I've got vacation time coming." He switched the phone to his other ear and drummed his fingers on his desk. He was nervous, impatient, half angry with himself, a little bewildered...and excited. Basically, wired.

"You're scheduled for Minneapolis in three weeks," Thelma said.

"Send Jackson," Steve replied.

"He's in Tucson."

"He'll be back."

"They want you."

A pause.

"What's going on, Carlisle?"

He rubbed his forehead and tapped his right foot.

"I told you, Thel. There are some things here that I want to take more time with."

"Your own time," she said.

"My own time."

She sighed and Steve could see her shaking her head, lighting another cigarette from a smoldering butt, inhaling deeply and blowing smoke at the ceiling. Thelma Grant, with her wig-orange beehive, tight designer jeans and diamonds so big and plentiful they passed for costume, was a tough old bird whom he adored. Thirteen years ago, she'd given an ignorant and eager kid from the Midwest a break, and he'd worked his tail off for her ever since.

"Well," he said. "What do you think?"

"I think—" she blew out more smoke "—that there's a whole helluva lot that you're not telling me. However, I know you wouldn't ask me for this if it wasn't important."

"No," he said, and that was true. Too bad he hadn't the foggiest idea why it *did* seem important.

"A month?" she asked.

"Maybe two."

Thelma groaned. "All right, Carlisle, I get the message. You're flakin' out on me for Lord knows how long. Fine. Great. Terrific." Another deep breath. Another puff of smoke. "Here's the deal. I'll

count on you when and if I see you. But don't expect
to come bopping in without notice and expect to go
right out on a job—''

He laughed. "I won't. Thanks, Thel."

"For what? Taking you off the payroll indefi-
nitely?''

"No." He sobered. "For understanding."

"The only thing I understand is that you're getting lazy in your old age. I'm warning you, Carlisle,
if you don't get your tail back here in decent time,
I'll..."

Thelma went on and Steve chuckled. She filled
him in on what was happening back East, and he
wondered what in the world he was doing sticking
around Chicago. But before he could allow Thelma's brusque chatter—and his own common sense—
to change his mind, he made his excuses and got off
the phone.

He didn't have time to analyze his motives.

He had more important things to do.

He had his own job to finish. And then he had a
magazine to help run.

Sarah was long accustomed to dragging home
stacks of work, but tonight—and probably every
night, from now until October twenty-fifth or there-
abouts, when the baby was due—she was carting a
mountain of it.

After the preliminaries were handled, she could delegate a lot. But her staff was small and Sarah was a perfectionist. On a project as important and exciting as this one, she wasn't going to take any chances at anything not getting done.

"Hey!" A male voice called from behind her. "Hey, you shouldn't be carrying all that." Steve rushed up and scooped the files out of her arms. Then he noticed that her straw carryall was stuffed to the gills and he grabbed that, too.

"I'm fine," Sarah said, but couldn't help feeling relieved by the absence of the load. "Really. I carry a ton of junk with me everywhere I go."

"Don't care," Steve said, shaking his head. "If I didn't carry a lady's parcels, my old granny might hear about it and take after me with a switch."

Sarah laughed, imagining that. "You sound like Huckleberry Finn. I'll bet you never had *any* old granny—how was it you put that?—take after you with a switch?"

He grinned wryly. "You'd lose that bet." He took her arm and steered toward her car. "My mother's family live in southern Alabama. Peanut farmers. I used to spend summers down there when I was a kid. Not only did she use a switch, she used a *green* switch, fresh cut. Talk about sting..."

"I can imagine," Sarah said, still grinning. "I bet that was quite an experience, wasn't it? I mean, going from New York to southern Alabama?"

He flashed her a look. "I'm not from New York. Not originally."

"No?" Sarah was surprised. Somehow he'd just seemed like the big-city type, born and raised.

He shook his head. "Iowa," he said. "Davenport, just a couple of hours from Chicago. I didn't go to New York until I got out of college."

"I just assumed," Sarah said.

"I know." His voice was dry. "You do that a lot."

They reached her car and she unlocked the doors. As he was stowing her stuff on the passenger side, he asked, "What is all this? Stuff for the new project?"

Sarah nodded. "Yep. And that's just the beginning."

He closed the passenger door and straightened. "You working tonight?"

Sarah smiled dryly. "I guess you weren't kidding when you said they call you Sherlock. You really don't miss a trick."

He tipped his head to the side and folded his arms across his chest. "Anybody ever tell you you have a real talent for sarcasm?"

"Every day, Carlisle," she said, opening the driver's door. "Every day."

He came around to her side of the car. "What time do you usually start?"

For no reason at all, Sarah stiffened, feeling defensive for the first time since she'd read his prospectus.

"Start what? Being sarcastic? I don't know, around 7:30 a.m., I guess. Right after my first cup of coffee. Before that, my mind doesn't work well enough to do anything but—"

"Working," he said, his gaze level and probing. "What time do you start working in the evenings?"

Sarah rubbed her belly with one hand and fiddled with her car keys with the other.

"I—I don't know. It varies." A change of subject suddenly seemed imperative. She wiped her damp forehead with a sweaty palm. "It's like an oven in here," she said. "Listen, I'm going to have to get going and turn the air on. These days I have absolutely no tolerance for heat." Not waiting for a response, she inserted the key and started the engine.

When she looked back up, Steve was studying her, frowning.

"You know I was going to offer to help you tonight," he said, making it sound like an accusation.

"I know," Sarah replied, looking down briefly. "And I appreciate that. It's just . . ."

"Look," Steve said. "When I offered to stay here and help out with *Midwest Woman*, you jumped at the idea. I had to rearrange a lot of schedules—not just mine—to make time for this. So if you want the help, fine. And if you don't, just say so."

Sarah looked up, startled. "You told me you had vacation time coming and wanted to stick around the area for a while anyway—to visit your family, spend time with Mark . . ."

He looked guilty for an instant, then grinned and shrugged. "So I lied."

Her face froze. She had heard enough pretty lies to last her a lifetime.

"I see."

"No, you don't." He leaned against the top of the opened door. "All of it was true," he said. "I do have vacation time coming—lots of it. And I do want to spend some time with my family while I'm here. But the main reason I'm staying is to help with *Midwest Woman*. That's the truth, Sarah. So if you don't plan on accepting my help, you need to clue me in right now. It'll make a difference."

Sarah stared straight ahead, wishing he hadn't told her this, hadn't put this decision all on her. *Of course* she wanted his help. He had a fabulous mind and was the creator of the Divine Plan. His input, at this stage, would be more valuable to her than anyone else's. But . . .

"I don't want you to stay just to help me."

"Why not?" he said easily.

"Why would you?" she challenged, turning to face him with a stony expression. "What's in it for you?"

His eyes narrowed, the way, she'd learned, they did when he was sizing her up.

"There's a lot in it for me," he said.

"Such as?"

"Such as…it's a challenge, and I've always loved a challenge."

"And?" She hoped there was more, because if not, it would mean he was only staying because he thought she couldn't handle it. If that were the case, Golden Boy Carlisle could just take a hike. She didn't need him. She didn't need anyone. Why couldn't people understand that and just leave her alone?

"And," he said, "it would be a new experience. I've never been directly involved in publishing and I'd like to get a more personal view of how things work. I'd learn a lot. Besides, I've always wanted to stick around and see my ideas come to fruition, but I've never had the time or the opportunity. Now, since it's my uncle's company and I'm due for a break, I have both. When I got to thinking about it, it just seemed too good a chance to pass up."

She was watching him, thinking, judging his reasons for merit.

His smile was more of a smirk. "Well? Satisfied?"

"I guess so," she said. His explanation seemed solid.

"You're too suspicious. You need to learn to lighten up."

The conversation was taking a turn, a *personal* turn, that she had no intention of pursuing. "I usually start working right after dinner. If you're free and you feel like working, the help will be appreciated." She leaned out, and grabbed the door handle. "Around seven, Carlisle. I'm in the book."

She smiled briefly, pulled the door shut and drove away.

Steve was whistling—and grinning—as he strolled toward his rented car.

Sarah couldn't sleep. She had one of those old, wind-up alarm clocks on her nightstand and the blasted ticking was keeping her awake.

5:45. Terrific. No nap in sight, and he'd be at the apartment by seven.

She growled in frustration and flopped onto her back. No good. The best position for blood flow to the baby was when she lay on her side, her *left* side, of course, which she'd never slept on in her life. She had wild fantasies about the day when she could once again sleep on her stomach.

It was no use. She was tired, but obviously much too keyed-up to sleep. It had been a big day, and the plans for the magazine were very exciting. She struggled and pushed and managed to get up.

The living room was a mess, so she straightened and dusted. She washed the few dishes in the sink and put them away. She made a pot of coffee, even though she couldn't drink any of it. She found a bag of cookies and put some on a plate.

6:15.

She fixed a salad and a bowl of vegetable soup and then ate it with bread and peanut butter—for protein—and a large glass of milk.

She hated milk, but drank it anyway, chugalugging it and thinking of her baby's strong bones and teeth.

She washed those dishes, brushed her teeth, and combed her hair.

6:35. And counting.

Her stomach churned and she had to throw up.

By the time she'd washed, changed, redone her makeup and calmed herself down, her doorbell was buzzing.

She went to let him in.

It was the first time she'd had a man in her apartment since Gary.

"Nice place," Steve said, looking around. He had changed from a suit to a pair of tan slacks and cream polo shirt. He stood in the middle of her living room, hands casually thrust in his pockets.

"Thanks," she said. "The stuff's in the kitchen."

"Stuff?"

"Files," she said. "Work."

"Oh."

She walked past him, to where a tiny kitchen was separated from the living room by a short bar with a butcher-block countertop.

Bemused by her lack of polite preliminaries, he grinned faintly and followed her lead. One thing about Ms. Sarah Jordan, he thought: she could never be boring. Her moods were too mercurial and unpredictable to lull a person into any sort of comfortable doze.

He remembered her talk and laughter and excitement from earlier that day and felt confident that such a mood and companionability could soon be restored. As soon as they got to work. With the often hard-nosed Sarah Jordan, work seemed to be the key.

"Have a seat," she said, and pulled out a kitchen chair for herself. "Oh, I made coffee."

"Sounds good," he said, maintaining that faint grin.

She started to push up from the chair, but he stopped her, rising quickly. "No, sit. I'll get it. Where are the cups?"

She pointed toward a cabinet and he took down two stoneware mugs. He wasn't surprised when he didn't find delicate china.

"Oh," she said, realizing his intentions. "None for me, thanks. I've already had my caffeine quota for the day."

"Ah." He grinned and replaced the cup. "I forgot. The baby. I remember when my sister Anne was pregnant and she had to kick the habit. She was a real cola-and-coffee junkie, but she's been off the stuff ever since."

"Decided she didn't need it, huh?"

"Not exactly." He filled his cup and carried it to the table. "She decided it was too hard to give up, and she didn't want to have to go through it again the next time. She's had three since—kids, that is."

Sarah gave in to a grin, but Steve was aware that it was strained. While she had rarely been fully comfortable around him, this tension tonight was of a different breed.

He knew it had everything to do with being out of the office, on private territory, where things could so often become more relaxed, less restrained. She was obviously determined that that wouldn't happen. He was just as determined to see that it did.

"Okay," he said, leaning on his elbows. "What have you got?"

He patiently endured ten more minutes of awkwardness and tension, and then it evaporated completely. As Sarah got lost in her work, she became animated and vocal, enthusiastic and...utterly charming. The transformation mesmerized him.

An hour sped by, then two, while they brain-stormed and argued and haggled and planned. As they came to solid decisions, Sarah made pages of notes. And yawned. There were purple shadows under her eyes and he thought she looked exhausted.

While she was jotting down some target dates, he got up to stretch. "It's nine o'clock," he said, pretending surprise. "Getting late."

"Hmm?" Sarah said, still engrossed in her notes. She was writing furiously, her head tipped to one side, dark hair tucked behind her ear and spilling down to just brush the top of her shoulder. Her white cotton maternity shift made her hair and eyes look that much darker.

He chuckled, enjoying watching her, wishing it wasn't time to leave. This had been a very cozy, very homey evening. He had enjoyed himself more than would have seemed possible or appropriate.

But she's such a mystery, he told himself. *An enigma, and she keeps revealing one layer of herself after another.*

So maybe that was it. Maybe that was the root of his continuing fascination with her.

Yeah. And maybe it was nothing more than the fact that every time he got near her, the blood ran hot and fast through his veins.

Despicable, he thought for the thousandth time and grimaced. But then again, as long as he didn't *act* on those feelings, maybe there was no harm in indulging himself in the too-rare sensations. They'd wear off in time, he was sure. And maybe therein lay the explanation for his desire to stay.

The feeling was harmless, futureless and fun. Revitalizing. Reminiscent of hot youth. When it wore off, he'd go back to New York, and Sarah would have never known the difference.

So no harm would be done. For now, his crazy, adolescent attraction, combined with the challenge of the magazine, the lure of his family and the prospect of a long-delayed vacation was too attractive a package to resist. Or to keep chiding himself about. This whole thing was a lark, an experience, and he was a fool if he didn't just relax and enjoy it.

She suddenly looked up, caught him staring. "You said something?"

He smiled, to wipe any of his thoughts from his face. "Nine o'clock," he said. "If I recall, that was my sister Shauna's bedtime."

"When she was pregnant, of course," Sarah said.

"Of course. Which really bugged her to no end. Before she got pregnant she was the family night owl—always up till three or four in the morning, sleeping till noon. The minute little Jason came in and started running things, she was sacked out on the couch by nine o'clock at night—every night, for the whole nine months. She hated that."

"I know how she felt," Sarah said. "I have to take naps to get through the day!" Then her huge eyes squinted at him. "Shauna, you said?"

He nodded.

"And the other one was...Anne?"

"Right you are. She's the baby of the bunch. Just turned...let's see. Thirty-two. Last month." He shook his head. "Boy, that doesn't seem possible. I still think of her as being thirteen, torn between loving horses and boys and always running around with skinned-up knees."

She leaned back in her chair. "How many sisters do you have, Carlisle?"

"Six," he said happily, leaning back against the counter.

"Six?" She stared at him. "What about brothers?"

"None." He pulled a rueful face. "And yes, before you ask, I played with a lot of dolls."

She laughed, letting her head drop back, then looked at him, smiling. "I don't think it hurts boys to play with dolls—or girls to play with trucks. Kids need a variety of experiences."

"Mmm. Maybe so, but I got my variety under duress. We lived out in the country, with no close neighbors, so if I didn't want to play alone, I had to do what *they* wanted." He gave himself a melodramatic shake, as if casting off bad memories. "It was miserable, Sarah, just miserable. Imagine the whole gang of them—six, remember—against me. The whole experience has left me totally traumatized.''

''I can see that,'' she said, her smile wide and dazzling, eyes sparkling with amusement. ''You're a regular basket case, Carlisle. I could tell that the minute you walked through my office door.''

''Mmm,'' he murmured lazily. ''And you were about as accurate about me as I was about you. Now if you want to talk seriously about being traumatized, all you have to do is remind me of that day in the parking lot and I *will* fall apart. I've been thinking about it and I'm pretty damned sure that I have never been so embarrassed in my life.''

''What day?'' Sarah frowned. ''I don't seem to recall what you're talking about.''

''Ah, yes,'' he said, snapping his fingers, remembering their agreement to start all over. ''That's right. I must have you confused with someone else. I've never made any stupid mistakes around you, now have I?''

Sarah stood up. ''Maybe not. But chin up, Carlisle, there's still time. And I have faith in you. I'm sure you'll manage to mess up yet.''

''Thanks,'' he said dryly, walking toward the door. ''Thanks a whole heck of a lot.'' *For a wonderful evening. For the way I can hardly wait until tomorrow....*

''Any time,'' Sarah said as she saw him out. ''What are partners for?''

When he had gone, Sarah closed the door and leaned back against it, her hands absently caressing the baby that was just beneath her too tight skin.

It moved. A strong, tiny hand or foot thumped under her palms, and she caught her breath, in awe of what was actually taking place within her body.

After a minute or so, the movement stopped. She waited, but there were no more flurries.

The complete silence of the apartment gradually penetrated her thoughts, stilling them to match her surroundings. The humming of the refrigerator grew into a loud, oppressive buzzing in her ears. She could hear her heartbeat in her head and was aware of the pattern of her own breathing.

She wrapped her arms tightly around her belly—her baby—and closed her eyes. Bit her lip. Felt the ache in her throat and knew she was going to cry.

"No," she said, and pushed herself away from the door. "No."

She breathed deeply and regained control.

She went to the kitchen, poured a large glass of milk, and used it to wash down a half dozen saltines. Half an hour later, unable to sleep, she called Diane. And told her about the new, exciting plans for *Midwest Woman*.

The next morning, Sarah sorted through her notes and files and got together a stack of stuff for Steve. She sent it, via messenger, to his office. The jobs were ones he could take home and work on alone.

Chapter Six

The previous week, Diane had moved all the junk away from the walls of the nursery, stowing toys, blankets and baby clothes neatly in the closet. She'd dragged the crib, tools, cans of paint and supplies into the center of the room, so Sarah wouldn't have to lift and tote when she was ready to paint.

Now it was Saturday morning, and Sarah was, at last, ready to paint. She had a lot of work to do on the magazine, but much of it was think work, and she could think just as well while running a roller as she could sitting down.

To avoid splattering good work, she knew she had to start at the top. She arranged the paint pan on a box atop a kitchen chair so she could keep the tiring business of bending and straightening to a minimum. Barefooted for a surer stance, she stood on a second kitchen chair, its back to her front where she could hold on to it, and stretched toward the ceiling.

She had barely gotten started when the doorbell buzzed.

Steve lounged, grinning, in the outer hallway, a sheaf of paperwork under one arm.

"Hello," he said. "Ready for work?"

"I . . ." Sarah hesitated. "Actually, I'm not working today."

He had walked in past her, but now he turned and frowned. "Say that again?" An eyebrow arched.

She shook her head. "I wasn't planning to work until later tonight."

He stared. "I'm shocked, Sarah. Really. I never thought I'd see the day when you'd grant yourself a whole day off." He grinned with approval. "I didn't know you had it in you."

Sarah folded her arms across her upper belly and gave him a wry look. "What are you doing here? That stuff I sent to you last Wednesday should have kept you busy for a long time."

"Ah," he said. "You were trying to get rid of me. That's what I thought."

Her mouth slanted. "I was trying to find the most efficient way to get the work done, that's all."

"Mmm." It was a skeptical sound. "Anyway, it's done." He turned and took the files to the kitchen, setting them on the table.

Wide-eyed, Sarah followed. "You *couldn't* have finished all that stuff."

"Did," he said. "Except for a few things that I had to consult with you about."

Sarah shook her head. "No. That's impossible. I didn't accomplish half as much..."

He grinned. "But *I* don't have to go to bed at nine o'clock. I've got several hours a day that you don't have. It adds up, productivity-wise."

Still stunned, she paged through the paperwork, shaking her head. Convinced at last, she put the stack on the bar with her completed work.

"Congratulations," she said.

He dipped his head in acceptance. "So, if you're not working, what are you doing today?"

"Oh, I'm working. Just not on the magazine." She held up her hands to show the paint smudges. "The nursery. I've put it off long enough."

He frowned. "You're *painting*? In your condition?"

Sarah laughed. "Of course. It isn't exactly grueling work." Although the bending and raising and reaching had pulled on her already strained back. But it was a small room. It wouldn't take too long.

"The fumes," he said. "You shouldn't be breathing those—"

"I have the window open. And besides, it's latex. Harmless. I checked."

He studied her. "Still doesn't sound like a good idea," he muttered, and turned to gaze off across the living room and down the hall. "What are you using to stand on?"

"A chair," she said, getting tired of this whole conversation. "Listen, I was just thinking about taking a break. Since you're here, we can talk about some of the stuff you needed to consult me about."

He pulled his gaze away from the hallway, his mind, hopefully, away from the extreme hazards of wielding a paint roller.

"Okay," he said, and pulled out a kitchen chair.

"Would you like something to drink? Coffee, ginger ale ... milk?"

"Milk?"

She laughed. "That's what I'm having. I force myself several times a day."

"Coffee would be great," he said, and a minute later, they went to work.

Her "break" lasted two hours, which flew by. They did not stop working because they were out of things to do, but because Steve started complaining about being hungry.

"It's one o'clock," he said, rising. "Let's go get something to eat."

"No," Sarah said. "Really. I can't. I have too much to do here, and...I'm not all that hungry." *Or all that comfortable....*

As long as they were working, things were okay, even better than just okay. Their minds worked splendidly together, complementing each other, the result being that enormous amounts of work got done in an amazingly short time.

But the moment they stopped working...it was a different story. Much as she appreciated his business input, she had no time for anything else.

"You're starved," Steve said. "I heard your stomach growl twenty minutes ago."

Sarah forced a laugh. "That wasn't hunger. That was a result of The Occupation. He or she keeps wiggling, moving everything around in there."

His gaze dropped to her stomach, eyes widening as he saw her belly move...roll, with the baby's gymnastics.

"Sarah...could I... Never mind." He grinned. "Are you sure you won't come and eat?"

Sarah bit her lower lip, wondering if she was about to make a huge mistake. While she certainly didn't want to invite any sort of familiarity, the expression on his face had been so awe filled, a reaction to which she could completely relate. It seemed kind of selfish not to allow him to—

No. She recognized that as rationalization. The truth of the matter was that *she* wanted to share the experience with someone who could appreciate the wonder. While she was known far and wide as someone who kept her personal thoughts and problems and feelings to herself, she felt no such compulsion for privacy when it came to the baby. She had to constantly restrain herself from babbling about it to the whole world.

She tipped her head to the side. "Go ahead," she said, and put his hand on her belly. "There."

His hand was warm and strong, and Sarah was jolted by the feelings that his touch sent through her. It wasn't anything for him personally, of course, just undefined longings that would never be fulfilled—the normal, natural longings of an expectant mother for the support and presence of the child's father. If, of course, the father had not been Gary.

The baby wiggled, and Steve's mouth dropped open. Then the baby kicked, and his eyes flashed up to meet hers. When the baby really got going, producing a short series of rapid-fire punches, Steve laughed with wonder and joy.

So did Sarah.

Then the laughter died, the baby quit moving. And Sarah felt awkward.

"Well," she said, shrugging. "I guess that's the end of the show."

Steve seemed reluctant, but removed his hand. "Wow," he said. "That was something. Could I see the nursery?" he asked.

"It's a mess."

"I don't mind."

"There's nothing to see," Sarah said.

"I'm just curious." He shrugged. "Haven't you realized yet that I'm curious about everything?"

Sarah gave in, and pointed down the hall. "That way," she said. "First door on the left."

He walked down the hall. Sarah stayed where she was.

"You call this a *nursery*?" Steve yelled.

Sarah rolled her eyes. First Diane, now him. Everyone was a critic.

"It's not done yet!" she called back, willing him to go home. If he'd leave, she'd be able to get the room done. Only trouble was, it was one o'clock and she'd worked through nap time. She yawned, knowing that that would have to come first.

"I'll say it's not done," Steve said, frowning as he reentered the living room. "When is that baby due?"

Sarah leaned against the door. "The twenty-fifth—of October."

"That's what—three or so weeks away?"

"Four," Sarah said. "Almost."

His mouth slanted. "Nothing like waiting till the last minute."

"I know. I've been busy. And sick. And tired. And trying to put my life back together after the divorce. All in all, Steve, things have been a little hectic."

Silence fell, and Sarah bit her lip. What was the matter with her? Why was she telling him this? She felt his gaze and couldn't meet it.

"It's been tough for you, I know," Steve said, softly, gently, the quality of his voice inviting confidences.

She had a sudden crazy urge to let everything spill out—the pain, the disillusionment, the fear of all that was to come, and how well she could handle it.

No! She could handle it. She could handle it all.

She met his gaze with proud eyes. "It's no big deal," she said, and straightened from the wall. She walked past him. "Sometimes I just get tired."

Steve cleared his throat. In an effort to restore the atmosphere to a lighter level, he said, "So how about the nursery? Why are you doing it yourself? Why didn't you just hire a painter to do the work?"

"I thought about it," she said. "But in case you didn't know, publishing is notorious for its lack of decent pay. I guess they figure all the glitz and glamor we get is payment enough."

He smiled, the old sparkle of humor returning to his eyes. "I guess so. You can't have it all, huh?"

"No," Sarah said softly. "You definitely can't have it all."

His eyes narrowed on her. A puzzle, that's what I am to him, Sarah thought. She could almost see him sorting her out in his head.

Well, good luck, buster. Because I'll be darned if I'm going to give you any more clues. Things have gotten about as personal here as they're going to get.

She turned and opened the door.

He tipped his head to the side. "Going somewhere?" he asked.

"*You're* going to lunch. You're starving, remember?"

"No." He shook his head. "Change of plans. *I'm* going to paint your baby's nursery." Without waiting for a response, he took off down the hall.

Sarah took off—waddled off—after him.

"Oh, no you're not, Carlisle! I can handle this all by myself...."

Her voice trailed off as she reached the archway.

Steve was busy pulling off his shirt.

Sarah blinked, stared.

He paused, white polo shirt half on and half off.

"Not to be rude here—or crude—but I just can't see letting propriety ruin a seventy-five-dollar shirt. Can you?"

He looked so frank, so guileless, Sarah had to laugh. "Let's just hope you don't have the same monetary attachments to the pants," she said dryly. Then she proceeded to let him know that she did not, but thank you just the same, need any help.

Short of throwing him out of her apartment, there was no stopping Steve from painting that room. She argued, she cajoled, she demanded, and all the while he painted away, rolling smooth, cream-white semigloss over ancient, putrid, institutional green.

Finally, she gave up, because she wasn't going to throw him out. No more than she would order...say, Diane Fitzgerald out of her home. Diane was a friend. Sarah bit her lip, realizing that Steve, like it or not, was becoming something of one, too.

Oh, he had made excuses for what he was doing, claiming that this arrangement was much more efficient. This way, with them both here, they could get the nursery done and talk business at the same time.

Yet Sarah knew that was bogus, and she was touched. And felt herself distinctly soften toward him. It seemed incredible that this man, who could have no ulterior motives that she could see—and she'd certainly *looked* for any—would take it upon himself to help her out.

That's what friends are for, Diane had told her time after time. *Sooner or later you're going to figure that out.*

"Hey," Steve said, glancing back over his shoulder. "Why don't you order us a pizza or something. Or barbecue. Or chicken. Whatever delivers."

"I could fix something. I've got—"

"Why bother? We've got enough to do."

"There's a deli up the street," she said. "And pizza. Which sounds better?"

"Anything. Whatever suits your pregnant fancy."

He shrugged and resumed work, and her gaze was drawn once again to the play of muscles across his back. She'd been watching for the last ten minutes as they flexed and bunched and stretched beneath taut and tanned skin. She couldn't help but appreciate the well-toned physique, nor did his half nudity embarrass her.

She wasn't a prude—far from it. And she had the definite advantage of knowing that there was absolutely no sexual interest on his part or her own. Which left her free to study and admire a strong, healthy body with the same detached appreciation she could grant to Michelangelo's *David*.

"Well?" he said, looking at her again. "What's it going to be?"

She blinked. "Mmm. Deli sounds good. What do you want?"

"Pastrami on rye, hot, with mustard. Make that two. By the time I get done here, I'll be ready to inhale it."

It was nutsy, he knew, but Steve was having the time of his life. There was something so relaxed and cozy and domestic about the scene, and it pleased him inordinately. Normally he was not a particularly domestic person. He didn't even have his own home and was not especially bothered by that. He was in New York so seldom, he just used Thelma's company apartment, moving in and out with two big suitcases. And when he was on a job, he lived in a hotel room.

His other stuff, the personal junk everyone collects throughout life, was at his sister Claire's, where she kept a room open for him in her six-bedroom house. *Stability,* Claire told him every time he visited. *Everyone has to have some stability. Until you get yourself some of your own, it'll have to be here. Second-best, I know, but better than nothing.*

And there was something to that, Steve knew. He liked having the knowledge that there was a place he could think of as home. Sort of home. A place where he could be involved with a family....

He paused in his work, suddenly wondering if that was the draw here, with Sarah. If his continuing attraction to her and enjoyment of doing "homey stuff" had anything at all to do with what she represented—domesticity at its finest.

A beautiful woman, about to deliver a child. Work to be done to make everything ready. A place for him, for a time, to take part in how the rest of the world lived, with no threat whatsoever. In a few weeks he'd be leaving. Sarah would have her life, and he'd have his, which he loved.

But in the meantime, he could enjoy this—and her—while it lasted.

He grinned and reloaded the roller.

And wondered if this was what you'd call having your cake and eating it, too.

The room was done and Sarah was dazzled. So fresh. So clean. So new.

So perfect for a brand-new little doll-baby.

"It's perfect," she said, grinning. "Thank you."

"You're welcome." But he was scowling. "I know it's none of my business, Sarah, but..."

Sarah raised an eyebrow. "But when has that ever stopped you, right?"

He laughed and rubbed his chin—and smeared paint all over it. "Right. The thing is, this doesn't look like much of a *baby's* room to me. I mean, come on, Sarah. White? You could have picked something babyish, like pink or blue or—"

"I didn't want my little boy to come home to a pink room," she said dryly. "Or vice versa."

"Oh," he said. "Well, what about yellow? Anything would be better than white." He cast another disparaging look about the room.

Sarah laughed. She couldn't believe he was that put out...that interested.

"I'm not going to leave it this way," she said. "After the baby's born and I know what gender it is, I'll custom-design it in blue or pink. And now that I've laid your mind to rest, come on, Carlisle. Lunch is here."

She left while he was cleaning up and putting on his shirt. They ate the sandwiches with wavy chips and kosher dills. And talked about work. Sarah, pleasantly drowsy and relaxed, put her feet up on a kitchen chair and indulged in cola to help wake her up. While he was here, she might as well take advantage of the opportunity to accomplish some business.

He finished his second sandwich, then snapped his fingers, remembering something.

"I almost forgot," he said, looking at his watch. "We're supposed to be somewhere this afternoon."

"We have an appointment?" Sarah frowned. "Where? You didn't mention anything to me."

"That's because I almost forgot." He got up, gathered their napkins, waxed-paper wrappers and other trash and dumped it in the garbage bag under the sink. "Come on," he said, motioning her to get up. "We don't want to be late."

Sarah forced herself to her feet, but she was still frowning. A business appointment on Saturday? But then, Steve Carlisle got things done. Still, it didn't seem very professional or courteous not to give her more than sixty seconds notice.

"I have to change," she said. "And put on some makeup."

"You look great," he said, shaking his head and heading for the door. "Just slip on some shoes and we can get going."

"Going where?" she demanded, because she chose to be the judge of whether or not she was appropriately dressed. "Where are we going and who are we meeting with?"

"I'm sorry, Sarah," he said, looking solemn. "If I told you that, it would ruin the surprise."

She chewed him out about his mysteriousness during the whole fifteen-minute drive.

Blithely ignoring this, Steve just smiled and drove to the nearest shopping mall. Still smiling, he steered her straight to the first department store and its baby section.

"Carlisle . . . what are we doing?"

"Decorating your nursery," he said, and asked the saleswoman where he could find unisex toys and stuff for the walls.

"But I already told you," Sarah said. "I'm going to do this after—"

"I know." Steve sorted through a collection of quilted fabric wall-hangings—bears and bunnies and rainbows and clouds. "And you can redecorate later if you want. But when you bring the kid home, I think he should have something to look at, don't you? I mean, you're not going to get out of the hospital and trot straight over to the mall. It'll probably be—what? Two or three weeks at least."

Sarah paused, thought about that and sighed. Did she want her baby to come home to a blank room? Would a baby that age even notice or care? Then she remembered some experiments she'd read about regarding infants and colors, designs, sounds, photographs. From day one, babies responded to everything around them.

"Actually," she said, "you might be right."

And that was all it took. The next hour was a crazy, laugh-filled kaleidoscope of stuffed Mickey Mouses, Teddy Beddy Bears, colorful clowns, fuzzy ducks. Music boxes hidden inside stuffed animals, baby-buggy planters, myriad mobiles and tri-balloon lamps.

Steve watched her closely, observing which things delighted her most, and kept track of the things he thought best himself. In the end, he carted armfuls of things to the counter and told the woman to ring it all up.

"Are you crazy!" Sarah said, and told the woman to stop. "I can't afford all of this! I'm only going to get a couple of things, and—"

He turned away from her and told the woman to ring everything up.

"No!" Sarah demanded.

"Yes."

"No—"

"Yes." He put his hands on Sarah's shoulders and looked into her dark, dark eyes. "Please. I'd like to do this. Tell the baby the stuff came from Uncle Steve."

"Why?" she asked, and blinked at him in a total kind of confusion that went straight to his gut. "Why would you want to do this for me?"

Because I love you, he thought, and was so shocked at himself, he could think of absolutely nothing to say.

Chapter Seven

It's because you feel sorry for me," Sarah insisted, mouth tight with final comprehension. "That's what all this stuff has been about. You're some kind of bleeding heart who likes to take on a charity case every once in a while and brighten up their lives."

"Sarah! No—" Steve became conscious of the curious looks of the saleswoman and steered Sarah over to a corner that afforded more privacy.

She yanked her arm away. "Don't touch me. And don't buy me things, and don't help me out around my house. In short, Golden Boy, don't even *think* about doing me any more favors."

She spun away and started to walk off. "Oh," she said. "I can find my own way home."

He rushed to catch up with her and wondered how everything so good had gone so wrong. "Sarah. Listen to me. I don't feel sorry for you. How could I? How could anybody?"

She looked at him, frowning. "What do you mean, how could anybody?"

She was thinking of Diane and too many others, who felt sorry for her all the time. She had not, until now, sensed that from him and was only beginning to realize how nice it had been not to be looked upon as an object of pity.

"Look at you!" he said. "You've got it all . . . a great job, a face men would kill for, a fabulous mind . . . a baby on the way."

"And no man," Sarah said flatly, unconvinced. "In everybody else's book, that seems to be the only thing that counts."

"I don't feel sorry for you," he said. "I'm sure the divorce was plenty rough—especially with a baby in the picture—and I *do* sympathize with your situation. It has to be harder doing everything on your own. But . . ." He held up a hand to stop her when it looked as if she might turn and leave. "But . . . my only reasons for wanting to be around you are selfish ones."

Sarah crossed her arms over her belly and tipped her head back to look up at him.

"Selfish," she repeated. "How so?"

He smiled ruefully and looked down at his shoes, then back at her. "I have a good time," he said. "When I'm with you, I enjoy myself."

She squinted, weighing his words. Then her mouth slanted. "Well, I can certainly understand that," she drawled. "I mean, everything we've ever done together has been so wildly entertaining."

"Not wild," he said. "If it was, I doubt that it would be so...enjoyable." He ran a hand through his hair and wondered how to explain—without explaining too much. "The thing is, Sarah, I'm on the road all the time. If I want wild and exciting, I can have it. What I can't have is all the normal stuff—you know, things like hanging around the house and working on a nursery. Or buying presents for a baby. I'm thirty-five years old, never been married, never been a father—"

"At least as far as you know," Sarah said, supplying the old macho yuk-yuk line with heavy sarcasm.

He shook his head, unamused. "I'd know," he said. "I'd make it my business to know."

And somehow, looking at him, Sarah believed him. She sighed, feeling her bitter outrage slide away.

"So you're saying that spending five hundred dollars on some stranger's kid gives you some vicarious paternal thrill."

He raised an eyebrow. "Well...yeah, I guess it does, sort of. But somehow the way I feel and the way you say it, it loses something in the translation. Sounds pretty stupid, doesn't it?"

But did it? Sarah wondered, running it through her mind. Did it sound stupid or phoney or sappily unbelievable?

She remembered his face when he'd wanted to feel the baby...and remembered the look in his eyes when she'd allowed him to feel it move. That pleasure had been real, no doubt about it.

In the past, before Gary, she remembered herself when she'd seen Diane with her kids. She remembered the sense of wanting that had been set off within her. She also remembered the presents she bought for Mark and Jana whenever she could.

But this was a man. A stranger.... *A friend,* a little voice reminded her.

Yes, a friend.

A friend who needed something that she was in a position to give during the time he was here. So while he was helping her, she was helping him in return. Just by allowing him to take part in her life.

Absurd as it sounded, bizarre as it felt, Sarah truly believed that, deep down where the feelings grew.

"I'm sorry, Steve," she said huskily. "It seems once again I've done you a disservice."

He grinned and shook his head. "No sweat, Jordan. I'm getting used to it. Now tell me. What's this 'Golden Boy' stuff all about?"

Chagrined that she had actually called him that aloud, Sarah let him steer her back toward the gawking saleswoman, explaining all the way.

In the end, they left the store with about half of his original selections, still a lot of stuff. Back at the apartment, Steve insisted she sit down and put her feet up on the old corduroy recliner while he brought everything in and fixed some iced drinks—ginger ale for her and cola for him.

When he brought the drinks, Sarah was asleep. Steve grinned, then sobered.

He loved this woman. Could that be true? Or was this just some passing—

No.

It was not. He didn't know how he knew that, but he knew. Too bad he didn't know what in the world he was going to do about it. Sarah was about as ready to let another man into her life as he was ready to abandon the career he'd worked so long and hard to build. Maybe other men with families were away from home for weeks at a time, but that would never sail with him.

Looking at Sarah, so relaxed and peaceful, her hand covering her growing infant, protective of it even in sleep, Steve thought for the first time about

Mark's offer of a job. President and CEO of Houston Publishing.

He had to admit that the idea was not without a certain appeal. In the last month or so he had learned a lot about the field and found it both interesting and exciting. Maybe he'd talk to Mark and find out a little more about it....

But that was crazy. Sarah wouldn't want him, or anyone, certainly not now and probably not in the near future. No matter what she said in words, she communicated so much in so many other ways. She'd been hurt badly. Trust for any man would be a long, long time in coming.

So could he feasibly live here in the same town, work for the same company, see her and know she was within reach but out of touch?

She was beginning, finally, to accept him as a friend. Would that be enough? And even if it was, how long could he keep his true feelings to himself? And he had to keep them to himself—for her sake. It was too soon. She was too vulnerable. Pushing her now would be taking unfair advantage.

He set her ginger ale on the end table next to her, then fought down the urge to just stay and watch her. Instead, he went to the nursery, found some tools and started putting together Sarah's baby's crib.

"Surprise!" Everyone shouted when Sarah walked into the cafeteria Monday morning.

She stopped, stunned, and looked around. Twenty-five or thirty women were standing there and grinning. Diane Fitzgerald came forward and pulled her into the room.

"What is this?" Sarah said.

"A baby shower, of course." Diane gestured toward a table teeming with white- and pastel-wrapped boxes.

"Diane, I told you . . ." Sarah stopped herself just in time from appearing totally ungracious. But she had told Diane months ago that she really did not want a shower. She wasn't very close to anyone, and inviting her co-workers to a shower seemed rather akin to begging for gifts, a repulsive thought.

"Tough cookies, Jordan. Since when did anybody make your word law?" Diane said. They hadn't quite reached the group, and Diane turned to face Sarah, her back to the rest of the women. Her smile faded and her expression was stern. "Look. Everybody *wanted* to do this, Sarah. I didn't force them. It just kept coming up, and pretty soon it was all planned. They care about you. They want to do something to make you happy. Now smile big and show them the same courtesy, hmm? If you can't do that and make it genuine, then fake it. It's the least you can do."

Sarah swallowed, shocked by Diane's anger. Did the woman really think she would be so rude, so callous, as to make everyone feel that she didn't appreciate their efforts?

Of course she appreciated this.

She was just so…surprised. So…uncomfortable. She was twenty-eight years old and had never had anyone to rely on but herself. By the time she was fourteen or fifteen, a fierce independence was already ingrained. Independence and wariness of others.

The independence had gained strength as her mother had weakened, succumbing to the alcoholic haze that finally killed her. The wariness had begun in grade school, when Sarah had invited Cindy Harper home to spend the night and the next day the whole school was talking about Sarah's mother, who had reminisced over endless vodka tonics before passing out on the ratty living room sofa. Talking…and laughing, and Sarah had never invited anyone to her home again.

There were other incidents as her mother deteriorated, along with an endless stream of her mother's boyfriends, several of which Sarah had had to fend off. She'd left home at sixteen, got a job and got her diploma through night school, then put herself through college. A loner, that was what she was, had always been, with the exception of her weeks with Gary. And, especially after that fiasco, she had determined that a loner was exactly what she was meant to be.

Yet suddenly her life seemed teeming with friendly faces, caring gestures, people who kept reaching out and—

An arm came around her shoulders. "Now this," Diane said, hugging her, "is rather overdoing it, don't you think?"

Sarah realized she was crying, something she'd done very rarely since the turbulent days of adolescence. Yet now, here she stood, making a fool of herself, *exposing* herself in a roomful of strangers she had known for years.

And she began to laugh. Because it all felt so very good.

"Happy baby, Sarah!" someone said. "What do you say we get to the presents?"

That day and the week that followed were some of the best, happiest days of her entire life. The plans for the magazine were fast becoming a reality, and she was thrilled about that. The nursery, with the items she'd picked up along the way, the things Steve had bought, the wonderful gifts from the shower— rattles, blankets and sleepers, diapers and pins and a blue plastic bathtub that fit securely on the kitchen sink—was complete, absolutely perfect in every way.

Steve came by every night except Thursday to work on the magazine, but they always ended up in the nursery. He'd put the crib together last Saturday afternoon, and set up the changing table she'd bought secondhand. During the week, they put up wall hangings, hung curtains, moved a chest of drawers out of Sarah's room and painted the old, scuffed-up thing—white, of course—and filled it with blankets and clothes.

As a grand finale, on Saturday afternoon, Steve had attached his favorite purchase to the crib. A musical mobile with four small fuzzy bears clutching colored beachballs that went round and round with the music. "A kid who can't even turn himself over has got to have something up there to keep him from getting bored out of his skull," Steve had said.

All in all, everything in her life was pretty terrific.

Now, all she had to do was wait, which was getting harder by the day. In approximately two-and-a-half weeks, she was going to be a mother.

With October came relief from the heat. The weather seemed to be watching the calendar and changed overnight. Instead of cotton shifts and blouses, Sarah wore maternity sweaters and pants, which she borrowed from Diane. She was wearing cream wool pants and a deep raspberry-colored sweater on Monday night, when Steve arrived.

He stopped just inside the door, looked her up and down and gave a long, low wolf whistle. "You look fabulous," he said, and actually looked as if he meant it.

"I look as big as my sofa," Sarah said, closing the door. "And I feel bigger." She was barefoot, as usual. Lately, none of her shoes fit comfortably except flat sandals and a pair of old sneakers.

"That color is great on you," Steve said, still staring.

There was something in his eyes that made her feel warm. She changed the subject and ushered him toward the kitchen. There was still so much work to get done on the magazine before the baby arrived. Two and a half weeks was not much time.

As she pulled out a chair and prepared to get down to business, a sort of *twanging* pain made her bend over.

"Sarah!" Steve said, alarmed. Instantly he was at her side. "What's wrong? What is it?"

Sarah smiled and eased up again. "Nothing. Just a few false labor pains. I've been getting them off and on for the last few weeks."

He helped her sit down and frowned at her nervously. "You're sure? You're absolutely positive this isn't the real thing?"

She shook her head. "Positive, Steve. The baby's not due for two and a half weeks. And most first babies come late, not early. At least that's what everybody keeps telling me. Personally, I hope mine will be born on schedule."

He grinned, but still seemed worried. "Are you sure you don't want to run over to the hospital and get this checked out?"

"No!" Sarah said, grinning. "This is perfectly normal. Besides, even when you really are in labor, you don't even *go* to the hospital until the pains are regular and about five minutes apart. Sit down, Golden Boy," she said, using the nickname that had since become a joke between them. "Relax. No, on second thought, don't relax. We've got an awful lot of work to do."

But an hour later, he saw her flinch again and knew she was having another one of those pains. It made him nervous and anxious for her, and beads of perspiration popped out on his upper lip and brow. How could she seem so calm about this, so blasted serene? He took a long breath and let it out slowly. The next couple of weeks were going to be nerve wreckers.

On Friday night, the twentieth of October, Steve took Sarah out to dinner to celebrate. Most of the crucial work for the magazine was finished. Contacts had been made, deals secured, arrangements and schedules established and confirmed. Together they had accomplished an enormous amount, and together they would celebrate the victory.

"Lobster," he told the waiter, refusing a menu. "For two."

Sarah didn't argue. Lately, she hadn't argued or questioned nearly so much as she had in the beginning. Her defenses had crumbled, almost completely. Steve knew she finally trusted him—as a friend—and reveled in the knowledge.

They'd had so many warm moments in the past couple of weeks. They'd discussed each other's backgrounds, families, hobbies, books, music, food. And while Sarah skirted around highly personal or emotional subjects, she had said enough for Steve to have put together a picture of her life. It had been hard from the start, with an alcoholic mother and a father who'd deserted them early on. First her father, then Gary. Steve could hardly blame her when she'd said she had no desire to get married again— ever. She'd have herself and her baby, and that would be more than enough.

He understood this, but knew it left him completely out in the cold.

But if she cared about him, even trusted him as a friend, why couldn't that just naturally develop into something more over time? Would she let it? Or would any hint of deeper feelings prompt her to cut all ties with him to avoid being hurt?

He sighed and gave himself a mental shake because he just didn't know. All he knew was that he desperately wanted to be with this woman all the time, and especially now so he could be there to help and to share in the arrival of her baby. *Our* baby, he had begun to think in the deepest, most private part of his mind. It was crazy, but he loved that kid and wanted to be able to show it.

"Hey, Golden Boy," Sarah said, tipping her head to the side. "We're supposed to be celebrating, remember? What's wrong?"

It was on the tip of his tongue to just tell her, but he caught himself. "Not a thing." He cut into his lobster tail, dipped it in drawn butter. "This is great," he said. "How's yours?"

"Perfect," Sarah said, but still looked concerned. "Are you sure nothing's wrong?"

"No. I was just thinking about...I was wondering if you've been having any more of those pains."

"A few," she admitted. "Two or three earlier today. But it's nothing. When labor hits, I have a feeling I'm going to know."

He nodded and speared more lobster. Yes, *she'd* know. She'd finished her childbirth classes last week and knew what to expect and when. So when the real labor started, she'd know. And unless he just happened to be there when it started, he *wouldn't* know. Sarah wouldn't call him. She'd call Diane.

Damn. This situation was untenable.

He *had* to be there with her, that was all there was to it. As the man who loved her, it was his place, his right! Well, maybe not his right at all, but that minor fact didn't change his desires.

He didn't want to just wake up one morning and find out it was all over with. He wanted to be there, be a part, even if it just meant pacing around in the expectant fathers' waiting room and handing out cigars. He just wanted to be close to Sarah from the minute the whole thing began.

That was the goal. Now all he had to do was figure out how to accomplish it.

They didn't talk much on the way home. Sarah rested her head on the seat back, relaxed and happy. A few days, just a few short days and all the waiting would be over.

"You're smiling," Steve said. "What are you thinking about?"

"The baby. What else." She turned her head to look at him, the straight, well-cut profile, the easy slouch he always relaxed into when driving or at her apartment. In the past weeks, he had become a rather important part of her life. He would be leaving soon, and she knew she was going to miss him.

"It won't be long now, will it?" he said. "Any day."

Sarah rubbed her belly. The baby had settled down recently, not moving as much as in previous weeks and months. That was normal, probably resting up for the huge ordeal of being born.

"Sarah," Steve said, glancing at her briefly. "When you go into labor, would you mind . . . you know, giving me a call to let me know?"

Sarah frowned. "No, Steve, I'm just going to go have my baby and not tell you a thing about it." She laughed, shaking her head. "After all you've done for this kid, I think I could manage to give you a call and let you know if it's a boy or a girl."

He was silent for a moment, but kept his eyes on the road. It was a cool night and clear, with a nice, light breeze.

"I meant," he began, "could you give me a call when you go to the hospital—when you go into labor."

Sarah's eyes widened. "I—I guess so. But why? It can take fifteen or twenty hours before anything happens. Or more. And it could be at two o'clock in the morning." He turned the car onto her street, then into a slot in the parking lot. "Look," she said. "Let me just call when the baby gets here. I—"

He switched off the ignition and turned to face her, taking one of her hands and holding it. For Sarah, the car suddenly seemed to get very small.

"Steve...."

"Sarah." He seemed about to say something, then changed his mind. "Come on," he said. "It's cool out here. Let's get you inside."

Her apartment was on the ground floor. He took her arm, as he always did these days, to ensure safe navigation. She unlocked the door and he poked his head in, listening and looking around.

"Looks safe," Sarah said dryly, but had to admit she was touched by his concern about possible intruders.

"Yeah," he said, and stood there in the hall.

She hadn't planned on inviting him in and he knew it. It was after eight and she went to bed early lately, knowing she needed to rest up for the big day.

"Thank you for dinner," she said, then decided a few more minutes wouldn't hurt. "Want to come in for coffee?"

He seemed tempted, but shook his head. "No. No, thanks. You better get some rest."

"Okay." She smiled, but this was beginning to feel awkward. Like it had in the car. Like he had something to say but was nervous about saying it.

Something, maybe, that she would *not* want to hear.

"Well..." she said, and shrugged, wishing he would leave.

"Well..." He blew out a short breath and grinned. "Good night."

"'Night."

He started to walk away. He took three or four steps and then abruptly stopped and spun around. He recrossed the distance before she had even moved to close the door.

"Sarah." Close now, he put his hands on her shoulders.

"What?" It was a husky sound. Her throat was tight.

He was looking down at her, mint-green eyes more intense than she'd ever seen them. *No,* she said to herself, not pursuing the thought beyond that. *No, no, no...*

"There's something I need to tell you," he said. "Maybe I shouldn't. Maybe I'm going to regret it. Maybe we're both going to regret it, but I don't think I can stand it anymore, so I guess I've got to take the chance."

No, her mind repeated dumbly.

"I love you," he said.

And Sarah's heart froze in her chest. Because she knew she had been betrayed.

Chapter Eight

"Go home," Sarah said woodenly, staring straight ahead. "Just...please. Go home." She backed away from the door, started to shut it.

"Sarah." Steve darted forward so she couldn't lock him out. "Wait. We need to talk."

His guts had dropped down into his shoes. He hadn't told a woman he loved her since he was sixteen. It wasn't an easy thing to do.

Instead of trying to stop him from coming in, she turned and walked away from him, slowly, like some automaton. Steve didn't like the way she was reacting; it scared him.

She went into the kitchen, mechanically poured a tall glass of milk.

"I'm sorry," he said. "I shouldn't have said anything—not now. Not until the baby is born and—"

She shrugged one shoulder, but didn't bother to look at him. "Doesn't matter," she said, and he doubted that anything could have stung him more.

"Doesn't *matter*? I pour out my deepest emotions to you and it doesn't matter?"

She looked at him, blankly, flatly. "Something had to happen to spoil things, didn't it? I mean, our relationship was really too good to be true."

He blinked, wondering if his last words had sunk in to her at all. "Sarah—"

"Only in fiction," she said, ignoring him. Then she gave him a brief, humorless smile. "That's something I say a lot, you know. Only in fiction. Sometimes it seems like that's the only place where really good things can happen—and last." She tipped her head to the side, looking down at her stomach. "Except this, of course. My baby. Now *that* is definitely a good thing."

This was bizarre. Steve watched her, shook his head, wondering what the hell was with this disjointed conversation. While he hadn't really expected her to receive his declaration with open joy, he definitely hadn't expected this. She didn't seem hurt. She didn't seem angry. She just seemed . . . robotic.

Expressionless, she finished the milk, then turned to rinse the glass and set it in the sink. She stayed that way, with her back to him. Steve felt almost relieved when her shoulders started to shake. She was going to cry, but at least that was something normal.

"Sarah—"

"I trusted you!" she shouted, and whirled to face him. *"Damn* you, Carlisle, I trusted you to be my friend. Do you know how hard that was for me? How *nice* it was after we got through all the rough parts? Now we have *nothing*, can't you see that? We have nothing."

"That isn't true," he said, surprised and shaken by the outburst and by the betrayed look in her huge dark eyes. "I'm still a friend. If nothing else, I'll always be that. I'll always care, Sarah—"

"No." She pushed away from the sink and walked past him into the living room. She went to the window and looked out at the parking lot.

He wanted to go to her and take her in his arms.

She cared for him, he knew that. Maybe—obviously—she was not wildly in love with him, but she did care, otherwise she wouldn't be so upset at the prospect of losing what they had.

"Let's forget it," he said. "Let's just put this behind us and go back to where we were. Start over. We've done that once before."

She dropped her head back and flexed her shoulders, trying to ease the tension. His hands itched to

knead the muscles in her back and neck and her legs
and feet, which got so sore these days. If she'd only
let him, he could be so good for her, make things as
easy as possible.

"Come on," he said. "Let's forget it."

She turned, slowly, and gave him a wry smile.
"You're crazy, Steve. Real life doesn't work that
way. It would never be the same, can't you see that?
We'd never be able to relax again, to forget. Neither
of us. Those three little words are always going to be
there—"

"Ruining things," he finished bitterly. Then his
eyes narrowed. "You know, I've never said that to a
woman before. I was always, I don't know, saving it,
I guess. Saving it for that one special woman, like it
was some big fat wonderful prize or something."

He laughed, but it was a bitter sound loaded with
irony and self-derision. "What an ass I am." Shaking his head, he walked to the door. "Good night,
Sarah. I'll talk to you on Monday about the final
details for the magazine. Have a good weekend. Oh,
and don't lose any sleep over this deal, huh? Really,
it isn't worth it."

She let him go, of course. But still, idiot that he
was, he walked slowly, hoping all the way to the
parking lot that she'd come after him, stop him, tell
him that she really had been in love with him all
along.

Right. And, as his Alabama grandmother would say, donkeys fly and chickens have lips.

Or as Ms. Sarah Jordan would say, things like that happen only in fiction.

Well, hurray. Everybody had their own personal saying to apply to his own personal hell. Wasn't that special.

He threw the car into gear and swung backward out of the slot. Then he floored the gas pedal and burned rented rubber getting out to the street. *Very mature, Carlisle,* an inner voice chided.

Sarah Jordan just didn't care about him, that was for sure. At least not enough. And not in the right way.

She was right. They could never go back. In a corner of his mind, he guessed he'd known that all along. He also guessed he'd known that it didn't matter because he'd never be able to go on with things the way they were. He'd made a final gambit, risking all to have it all . . . and lost.

Maybe he should have waited until after the baby, but then, that had been part of the gamble. If she'd responded favorably, he could have held that baby as a father. They could have started out from day one as a family, complete, with none of the parties involved missing out on anything.

It would have been great.

Now, of course, it would be nothing.

He wouldn't go to see Sarah when the baby was born. He wouldn't do that to her. After tonight, just seeing him would be difficult for her, awkward and stressful and problematic. He'd leave her in peace, let her bask in the warm joy of her child, and then...

And then—what?

The future came to him and answered that question. *And then, nothing,* at least as far as Sarah and her baby and Chicago were concerned. He didn't live here. He didn't belong. He had just been doing a job, and now, save for details, the job was done.

By the time he got to his hotel, he'd made up his mind. He called his sister Claire, told her to expect him in a couple of hours, then threw his clothes into his suitcases and carried them down to the car.

It was ten o'clock now. He'd be at Claire's around midnight. After a couple of days with his family, he'd be back in New York. Where he belonged.

The pains were stronger now, different from the ones she'd had off and on all day. And becoming more and more regular. As another one hit, Sarah sucked in her breath and doubled over.

The doorbell buzzed.

It took her a full minute to catch her breath and waddle to the door.

It was Steve, and Sarah thought she'd never been so glad to see anybody in her life.

"Come in," she said, and reached for his hand. "I'm so glad you came back."

"You are?" He seemed wary, stiff and reserved as he allowed himself to be tugged inside.

"I'm sorry," she said, looking up at him earnestly. "I was completely insensitive earlier. I know I hurt you, and...I'm sorry. I hope you'll accept that."

He was frowning. "Of course. Sarah, I'm not sure I know what this means."

She smiled, wanting to get all this over with so she could tell him about the baby. This was it, these pains were the real thing, she was sure. And now Steve was back, and once they sorted everything out, she could share her joy and excitement and fear with him, her valued friend.

"It means I think I understand what happened here...between us."

"You do." His eyes were narrowed.

"Yes." She half turned toward the kitchen. "Come on. I'll put on some coffee and we can talk about it, sort everything out." And then, in a few hours or whenever the pains were close and regular, they'd go to the hospital. Together. Sarah smiled at the thought.

But Steve wasn't smiling or following her to the kitchen. "I don't see what there is to sort out," he said. "I told you how I feel. What I need to know is how you feel."

She smiled patiently. "I care about you very much. I feel very lucky to have gotten to know you." She walked back over to him, wondering how to explain what she knew had happened.

"Look, Steve. We've spent a lot of time together these past weeks. We've had our...differences, and we've had our good times."

"A lot of good times," he said. "We could have more."

"And we will," Sarah said. "You and me and the baby. I don't want that to change." She held up a hand when he started to say something. "I know I said that things could never be the same between us, but I was wrong. I didn't...think, I guess. I didn't understand."

"Understand *what*?" he said. "I thought I made myself perfectly clear. I love you, Sarah. I love your child. I want to marry you, both of you."

"No," she said, shaking her head and smiling tenderly. "That isn't what you want at all."

He stared at her, saying nothing.

"You're not in love with me," Sarah said softly. "You're just in love with the whole idea of it, everything I represent. You said it yourself the other day at the mall. You don't get to do all the homey stuff very often. Then, when we started spending so much time together, you just sort of got caught up in it all, me...the baby.... Do you see what I'm trying to say?"

Steve looked at her, saw the hope in her eyes and died a little. She cherished their friendship and wanted so much to believe that she'd found a way to salvage it, to forget all his ardent declarations and go on as before. Which was what he'd thought he'd wanted, too, a couple of hours ago.

But was it?

This was his chance, his big opportunity to once again become a part of her life. All he had to do was lie through his teeth and renounce his feelings for her.

"Sarah . . . I—I just came back tonight to say goodbye." And he was still going to say it, *had* to say it. Sarah had been right. They couldn't go back. At least he couldn't. He loved her, and he couldn't go on seeing her and pretending.

"Goodbye?" She frowned. "What do you mean, 'goodbye'?"

"I'm on my way out of town. I've stayed too long. I've got a job waiting and—"

"No!" she said. "You're leaving because of me, aren't you? Because of what I said earlier?"

"No," he said, and lied to her for the first time. He smiled, to appear more convincing. "Look, you were right about one thing. I did get caught up—in the magazine, the baby, you. And it's all been great. But I've stayed too long. Really. They need me back in New York." He laughed, but felt ripped apart inside. "Or at least I *hope* they need me. I—"

Sarah was hugging herself, arms wrapped around her belly. "I don't believe you," she said. "This is too sudden. You didn't mention anything about leaving when you were here earlier this evening."

He couldn't lie to her anymore. "I just decided," he said. "I think it's for the best."

She looked hurt, then her dark eyes narrowed in accusation. "Didn't you listen to anything I said? Nothing has changed between us. You are not in love with me. Good heavens, Steve, how could you be?"

She turned away, walked to the window. "There has been nothing even vaguely romantic between us," she said firmly, forcefully, and for one tiny second she wondered if she was trying to convince him or herself. "We've been friends, co-workers, nothing more." It was imperative that he see that, because love . . . she couldn't deal with right now. She turned to face him. "Steve, love—the kind of love you're talking about—consists of more than just affection."

"I know," he said quietly. "It consists of a lot of things. Caring. Respect. Intimacy. Chemistry. Physical, mental and spiritual attraction—"

"You can't be attracted to me," she said, avoiding him with her eyes. "Not physically—not now."

"I am," he said simply, glad to finally be able to discuss it.

"That's impossible! *Look* at me!"

"I have. Nearly every day for the past six weeks. I like what I see, Sarah. Every inch of it. You have no idea how hard it's been for me to keep from showing you that."

"No." She shook her head. "It's like I said. You're just in love with the idea of—"

"Stop it," he said. "I'm not some teenager who doesn't understand his own feelings. I've been over and over and over it in my mind and I know what I feel. You don't have to like it, but you might as well accept it."

"Steve, you just—"

"Don't you think," he interrupted harshly, "that if I had just been in love with the idea of domesticity that I couldn't have found someone to marry me long before this? Do you really think that I would have deliberately chosen someone in your situation, someone who is so damned difficult to get close to, if all I wanted was to settle down and it didn't matter who with? And do you really, honestly believe that I would have tried so damned hard if I was in love with an *idea* rather than a woman?"

Sarah stared, wide-eyed, then swallowed as his words sank in.

"I guess not," she said, and looked at the floor. "I guess I was wrong."

And the fact that she was so obviously depressed by the idea of his loving her tore him apart.

"I've got to go," he said, wanting to shake her for what she was doing to him—to them and all they could have. To shake her or take her in his arms and kiss some sense into her. If he could just touch her, just hold her, maybe she'd realize she felt something more than sisterly affection for him, too. Or maybe she wouldn't. Maybe for her, the chemistry just wasn't there.

Either way, it was impossible to find out. He would do nothing to upset her any further.

"I'm sorry," he said. "I hope this hasn't been too upsetting for you. You don't need problems right now, you need rest."

He smiled, to show that there weren't any hard feelings. He'd had a second chance and opted not to take it. If she couldn't accept what he offered and he couldn't accept what she offered, then he'd just have to learn to live with that.

He crossed the room and took her hands. They felt like ice. "Take care, Sarah. Be happy."

He raised her fingers to his mouth, pressed a kiss on each hand. "I'm sorry I couldn't be what you wanted me to be, but know this. I will *always* be your friend. And if you ever, *ever* need anything at all, I want you to call me. If I'm across the country or halfway around the world, it won't matter. I'll be there for you, on the very next plane."

He meant it, Sarah thought, staring at him. He honestly, fervently meant it. No matter what happened, and even though she'd hurt him badly and let him know that she could never love him, he'd promised to be there for her if ever she wanted or needed him.

He was crazy, that was all there was to it.

No... he was honest and honorable and fairly built of integrity.

He loved her, and whether she returned it or not, that feeling would not go away. Unlike Gary, who had "loved" her until the fun wore off, this man loved her when there really hadn't been any fun. No real fun, no parties, no excitement ... no sex or even any possibility of that for many weeks to come.

If this wasn't the real thing, Sarah didn't know what was.

She began to tremble and had to bite her lip because of the strength of the emotions welling up inside her. Never in her life had anybody loved her so selflessly, so completely. Not even her own mother. She had honestly not thought this kind of love possible. Real people were basically selfish, giving in order to get, walking out when things got difficult, tossing yesterday's commitments out with today's rotting trash.

Yet ... that suddenly did not seem to be strictly true.

Only in fiction?

She looked into his eyes, looking for lies.

Saw truth, naked and hurting.

Looking for lack of depth or sincerity.

Saw an ocean, fathoms deep, filled with bitter-sweet pain.

And love.

The kind that didn't dissolve and blow away.

The kind that could be there for her forever, if she could just somehow accept it.

Trust it, because that was, after all, the bottom line.

Could she, did she, want to trust someone—any-one—with the only thing she had left—herself?

No! Never. She was all alone and she was making it, damn it, *making* it, and doing all right.

All right. Was that enough? The alternative, the prospect of real happiness—having someone to share and care and love and cry with—was about to walk out the door.

"Steve, I—" She swallowed. "Don't go."

He looked at her for a long moment. "Why?" he asked.

But she couldn't say what he wanted to hear. She wasn't ready yet. Not now. Maybe…maybe not ever.

"At least," she said. "At least stay until the baby is born."

"Sarah, I don't think—"

"You said if I ever needed anything, I could ask. I'm asking. Besides, it won't be too long. Surely you can stick around just one more day."

It took a moment for that to sink in. Then his eyes widened and his gaze flew to her belly. "You mean...?"

She nodded. "This is it. The moment we've all been waiting for."

After that, the tensions of the past hours dropped away, replaced by new ones, and by excitement.

"Sit down," Steve said, rushing her to a chair. "Wait, no, don't sit down. We've got to get you to the hospital."

"It's not time yet," Sarah said, smiling. Her pains were still very far apart. She hadn't even had one in the fifteen or so minutes since Steve had arrived.

"Where's your bag?" he said, green eyes scanning the living room. "Is it packed?"

"Packed and ready to go." Sarah lowered herself into the recliner and put her feet up. It had been a long day and was going to be an even longer night. If she could rest, it would definitely be to her advantage.

"Sit down, Carlisle," she said, feeling amazingly calm...and somewhat smug. This was it! She was on the verge of accomplishing something truly incredible. "Relax. This is going to take hours."

He was frowning, running his hands through his sunstreaked hair, looking around in agitation for something to do. "I can't relax," he said. "I've never had a baby before!"

Sarah grinned wryly. "And you aren't going to have one now. You're just going to calm down and help me, right? Isn't that what you're here for?"

He blinked, bit his lower lip, took a few long breaths. "Right. What do you want me to do?"

"Sit," she said. "Help me pass the time."

He had just forced himself to settle down on the couch when another cramp hit Sarah. She flinched, and he jumped to her side.

"Sarah?"

She clutched at his hand, holding tight, concentrating on how glad she was for his presence to take her mind off the pain.

Self-hypnosis, that's what natural childbirth was all about. Concentrate on breathing, concentrate on a favorite photograph, concentrate on your mate's face and how the two of you love each other and your baby so very much. But no, that last bit of advice was for couples, not her. Not for her and Steve.

She clenched her teeth as the pain peaked. Held on to him. Met his eyes. Saw the love and worry and concern. Knew she loved this man and never wanted him to leave.

The pain passed, fading slowly, the way it had grown. Her grip lessened, but she didn't let go.

"Okay?" he asked, putting a hand to her cheek.

"Okay." She nodded, smiled weakly and leaned back in the chair.

She had to rest. Had to think, about Steve . . . and her. And how she knew she must have loved him for a very long time—not minutes, not days, but weeks—and hadn't been able to see it. She loved him. Needed him. Wanted him so much it hurt.

But no. . . . No. That pain was the baby kicking. Her body and emotions were entangled. Another pain hit, and she recognized confusion in her head . . . in her heart. Love? No. She couldn't be in love. This was the pain talking. The fear. The need to not be left alone.

"What can I do for you," Steve asked, kneeling beside her. "Just tell me, Sarah. Tell me what to do."

Love me, she thought, eyes drifting closed. *Love me like they do in sappy movies and books. Love me . . . and make me know deep down that you'll never, ever leave me.*

But what she said was, "Call Diane."

Chapter Nine

He called Diane and he called the hospital and he called Sarah's doctor. After that, he decided it was time to go.

"But it's not time yet," Sarah said. "The pains are still fifteen minutes apart."

"I don't care," he said. "We're not going to take any chances."

"But—"

"We're going. Where's your bag?"

She sighed and pushed herself out of the chair. She looked so tired, and Steve wondered how she was going to be able to manage all that was ahead of her.

"Okay," she said. "Fine. We'll go. Obviously I'm not going to get any peace until we get to the hospital. The bag is in the bedroom. I'll get my coat."

They didn't talk much on the way to the hospital. Steve was immersed in driving quickly but safely. Sarah was immersed in too many thoughts to even sort out. She had two more pains during the drive, and with each one she noticed that he pushed the car just a little bit faster.

Diane was waiting when they arrived.

"Sarah! How are you doing? How far apart are the contractions?"

"Still fifteen minutes," Sarah said. "I shouldn't be here yet, but Golden Boy over there was too nervous to hang around the house and wait."

She gestured toward Steve, who had immediately gone to the desk to inform them of Sarah's condition.

Diane's gaze went to Steve, then came back to Sarah, a thousand questions in those deep blue eyes. Questions Sarah knew she was dying to ask, but wouldn't, not now, not until after the baby was born.

"He's been coming over almost every night," Sarah supplied.

While she'd told Diane he was helping with the magazine, she'd never quite gotten around to mentioning that he came to the apartment. Or that he decorated the nursery.

Or took her out to dinner sometimes.

Or shopped for the baby.

Or that he loved her. But that last bit she had only found out tonight.

"I see," Diane said, and tried to look casual about the news. But there was a new sparkle in her eyes, a hope, an expectancy that she didn't dare voice.

"He wants me to marry him," Sarah said, surprised at herself for sharing this. What had happened to the woman who kept everything private and personal inside?

"Oh, Sarah! I'm so happy for you."

"I said no—" The explanation was stopped by another contraction.

Diane led her to an orange molded-plastic chair. By the time the contraction had faded, Steve was back with forms for Sarah to sign.

After that, they were kept busy with the process of admitting and getting Sarah settled in her room.

It was the longest night of his life.

He sat for hours, watching Sarah go through pain that got progressively worse. By 2:00 a.m., the contractions seemed like they must be unbearable.

Three minutes apart, it seemed they barely gave her time to catch her breath in between before starting in again. She clenched her teeth. Tears streamed down her cheeks and sweat drenched her.

Yet Sarah endured.

And Steve was in awe.

He'd known childbirth was rough, but he'd never imagined it would be like this. Watching her, he wondered where anyone had ever got the idea that women were soft.

They were beside her all the time, Diane on one side of the bed and he on the other, holding her hands, feeding Sarah ice chips, wiping her face and neck with cool, damp cloths. And helping her get up and walk, when she couldn't stand lying down anymore.

It was a big, comfortable room. Provided everything went well, Sarah would labor, deliver and recover all in the same room, the same bed.

The idea was to provide a homelike atmosphere, where family and friends could be present during labor—or delivery, if the mother so desired. Steve knew that when it came time for that, he'd be expected to leave. But that was okay. Delivery was quick, concentrated. It was the long, agonizing hours leading up to it where he could be useful to her.

"Oh-h-h," Sarah groaned, catching her breath at another contraction.

"Breathe," Diane said, and began coaching her through it. Short breaths, long breaths, combinations of both.

Finally, the pain was gone and Sarah sank back into the pillows. Her eyes closed. She fell immediately into exhausted sleep.

Diane's eyes met Steve's across the bed.

She smiled. "Don't look so worried. She's okay."

He shook his head. "I never knew it was like this."

"Most men don't. It does them good to see, don't you think?"

He blew out a breath. "In a way, I guess. But it sure plays hell with your nerves to see somebody in so much pain."

"Especially when you really care, hmm?" Diane said, and gently withdrew her hand from Sarah's, careful not to disturb her. "The cafeteria reopened at two," she said. "I'm going to run down and get some coffee. Can I bring you something?"

"Coffee would be great."

"How about a sandwich or something to keep up your strength? It's going to be a very long night."

He shook his head. "Just coffee, thanks. I don't think I could keep anything down when she's going through this. Every time a contraction starts, my guts just—" He made a slow, tight fist to illustrate.

"Sympathy pains." Diane smiled in understanding. "It happens. My husband had sympathy morning sickness with our first baby."

"You're kidding."

"Scout's honor. Every day at ten o'clock, I went to throw up—and so did he. The guys at his office have never let him live it down."

Steve was shaking his head as Diane left, smiling a little at what he had learned. Then Sarah groaned and opened her eyes. Her hand tightened on his.

"Ice," she whispered roughly.

Her lips, her so-soft, so-beautiful lips were cracked and dry.

"Here." He held the cup of ice chips to her mouth.

She sighed, laid back, closed her eyes. "So tired," she said. A few minutes later, more pain began.

As labor progressed, nurses and doctors checked in more frequently. They attached a fetal monitor to keep track of what was happening to the baby.

At 5:00 a.m., the heartbeat was strong and everything looked good. The contractions were horrendous, less than two minutes apart.

"Can't you do something for her?" Steve demanded, of the calm, patiently smiling nurse. Diane was out in the hall, talking to the doctor.

"It's almost over now," the nurse said, and patted Sarah's leg. "You're doing beautifully, Sarah. Just hang in there."

And then she was gone and Steve ground his teeth. Sweat was streaming off him, too, now, soaking his clothes. He wiped his brow with his forearm and pressed a cool cloth to Sarah's face.

She was between contractions, resting, but opened her eyes. "It's okay," she said. "If I can't stand it, I'll ask for medication. But I don't . . . want it. The baby . . ." Exhaustion claimed her again and she was asleep.

She was incredible.

Steve felt dwarfed by her strength and courage.

"I love you," he whispered. "I love you so much."

She didn't answer, of course. But Steve could have sworn he felt her fingers tighten on his in response.

He squeezed his eyes shut, shook his head, knowing what he'd felt was only the result of wishful thinking.

7:15.

Contractions fast and furious.

Hard and brutal.

Sarah screamed.

Sometimes the pain and exhaustion pushed Sarah over the edge and made her completely incoherent.

Steve gripped her hand and stroked her hair and was terrified she was going to die.

"Push," Sarah said, gritting her teeth. "I... need... to... *push*!"

A nurse left, came right back.

"Okay," the doctor said, briskly entering the room. "This is it, boys and girls. We've got a baby ready to be born."

Sarah laughed and cried and gasped in pain.

Steve got to his feet, knowing she wanted him to leave.

But her grip on his hand was as iron-hard as it had been for hours.

"Sarah," he said. "It's time."

"Don't go," she said. "Please don't leave me."

It happened so fast.

One minute the doctor was telling her to push, push, push.

The next minute, Sarah was screaming in agony.

The next minute was the most beautiful and incredible of Steve's entire life.

The doctor held up a squirming, red-faced infant.

They cut the cord, suctioned nose and mouth, and the baby wailed, tiny face scrunched up in fury and bewilderment, little fists and feet flailing in the air.

Sarah was laughing and crying and reaching for her baby, while the nurses and doctors worked on her, finishing up whatever had to be done.

"Look at her, Steve! Oh, just look at her!"

But he could barely see her through the salty sting in his eyes.

His throat was too choked to speak.

As the nurse gave the baby to Sarah, he just stood next to mother and daughter and gawked.

"She's so beautiful," he finally managed, his voice rough and husky.

"Alexandra," Sarah said, trembling, crying, stroking the tiny cheek. "Princess Alexandra."

"Yes," Steve said. "Princess Alexandra."

It was a supreme moment, one that would stand out in his mind for all time. At that moment, he felt that if he never had anything else, this would have been enough.

Then the nurse gently pried the baby away and took her to the nursery, to weigh her, wash her and give her mother time to rest and recover.

The room emptied, and it was several minutes before Steve or Sarah noticed that Diane had slipped out with the doctor and nurses, leaving them alone.

"I was so scared for you," Steve said, sitting on the edge of the bed, holding both her hands.

"I was pretty scared for me, too," Sarah said, smiling but heavy-eyed. "It was worth it, Steve. Oh, was it worth it. Did you *look* at her? Isn't she incredible?"

He nodded, blasted eyes filling up again. "Too beautiful for words," he said. "So are you."

Her smile faded and she searched his eyes, then avoided them.

Steve could have killed himself for dragging her mind from the joy of the moment to the problems his feelings for her presented.

"Steve..."

Before she could tell him again that there was no future for them as man and wife, he sought to steer the attention back to where it belonged. To Sarah. To her baby. He had been allowed to share this with them and was grateful. But he also knew that none of this meant he was actually a part of them, or ever would be.

He stayed a few more minutes, until Sarah fell asleep. An hour of rest, and then she would be moved to a regular room.

He took the elevator down to the basement and found the cafeteria. He was tired and excited and joyous . . . and sad.

And hungry, he thought, trying to concentrate on the present. Sarah, safely through childbirth. The baby, perfect and healthy and beautiful. These were the things that existed now, things he could count on. The future . . . well, the future was something he didn't even want to consider.

How could he leave?

Yet . . . how could he stay?

"Steve!" someone said, off to his left.

Diane Fitzgerald waved to him from a corner table.

He nodded to acknowledge her, then went through the food line, getting scrambled eggs, ham, some biscuits and coffee.

He paid for the meal and joined Diane.

They had just spent a very long, very emotional night together. They had shared an experience that was about as personal as an experience could get. And it had seemed perfectly natural, at the time.

Now, however, he felt awkward, embarrassed somehow. He realized as he sat down that he barely knew this woman at all.

"Sarah okay?" Diane asked.

He nodded, looking mostly at his plate. "Fine. She's sleeping. They're going to move her to a regular room pretty soon."

Now Diane nodded and looked as if she was trying to think of something to say. Obviously the discomfort existed on both sides.

"The baby's beautiful," Diane said.

"Mmm." Steve finished chewing, swallowed. "Incredibly so." He took a drink of coffee, wishing he'd sat by himself. No, wishing he could be up there now, with Sarah.

Across the table, the blonde took a deep breath and let it out. "Look, Steve, I'm about to get into something here that is none of my business, but I just wanted to say..."

He met her eyes warily, held her gaze. "Yes?"

"I just wanted to say...don't give up on her."

He raised one eyebrow. "Sarah?"

She nodded, fiddled with the handle of her coffee cup. "Sarah is...not an easy person to get to know."

"Tell me," he said, grinning wryly, remembering those first couple of times they'd met. In her office, where he'd been so damned attracted to her he could barely think. In the parking lot, when he'd asked her to lunch, not knowing she was expecting.

Oh, the looks those brown eyes could give. Hot ice. Disgust. Loathing of men of "his type."

Then later, so gradually, the softening, the melting. The discovery of her true self unfolded one thin layer at a time.

"I love her," he said. Obviously Diane knew. "I'm crazy about her."

"I know. It shows."

"She doesn't feel the same way," he said. "About me, I mean."

"Give her time," Diane said. "She's been through a lot in the last year."

"I know," he said. "And I'd be willing to give her all the time in the world. But now that she knows how I feel...well, suffice it to say, things have changed." He remembered the look of betrayal, hurt and, finally, resignation when he'd told her how he felt. Remembered her saying *we had so much. And now we have nothing.* "I'm going back to New York," he said. "I think it's for the best all the way around."

"No!" Diane stared. "You can't leave. Not after last night. Sarah cares about you very much. She has to. No woman would allow—"

He rolled his head backward, then side to side, easing the kinks. "Last night was an exception. She was in labor. I was there. She didn't want to be alone."

"*I* was there," Diane said, leaning forward on her elbows. "She wouldn't have been alone. But she wanted you. She didn't want you to leave."

Please don't leave me, Sarah had said, right before she'd delivered.

And then, after the baby was born, she had talked only to him. *Oh, Steve, look at her! Isn't she beautiful!*

She hadn't even noticed when Diane had slipped out of the room.

He shook his head, to clear it of false hope. Because he also remembered her eyes when he'd said she was beautiful, too.

The sobering that reflected no pleasure, no comfort at his words.

The low quaver in her voice when she'd said his name, and he'd known she was about to tell him one more time that his attempts to go beyond friendship were ruining everything.

"She was scared," he said. "And exhausted. And half incoherent. You can bet that once she's rested, she's going to regret having had me there. Whatever happened last night happened in the heat of the moment. I'm her friend, Diane. Nothing more." He pushed back his chair, glanced at his watch. "If you'll excuse me, I want to go see if she's awake yet."

He desperately wanted to get away from this woman who kept trying to encourage him about something that was simply not going to be.

The last thing he needed right now was hope, false and foolish.

* * *

"My baby," Sarah said, before she was even fully awake. "I want to see my baby."

"And you will," the motherly, middle-aged nurse said. "Just as soon as we get you settled in your new room."

It seemed to take forever.

Sarah was nervous, anxious, impatient, as they made the switch, wheeled her down the hall and got her into her new bed.

Steve was there, but stepped out while she got settled and checked one more time.

"There," the nurse said, looking around. "Now here's a pitcher of water. I'll be back in a couple of minutes with some ice. Anything else you need?"

"My baby," Sarah said, exhausted but bristling with impatience. After nine months of waiting, this seemed ridiculous and cruel. "I just want my baby."

The nurse smiled, and picked up the phone. "Mrs. Jordan would like to see her daughter now."

Sarah finally relaxed, convinced now that there wasn't some cruel conspiracy going on. "Thank you," she said.

"It'll probably take ten or fifteen minutes," the nurse said. "Usually does. Whenever you want to see her, just call the nursery."

She left, and there was a tap at the door.

"Come in!"

Steve walked into the room, carrying a big white bear festooned with a pink-and-white ribbon with It's a Girl! lettered in gold. In his other hand was a small vase of pink and white roses.

Sarah laughed, smelled the flowers, hugged the bear.

"Thank you," she said. "Thank you... for everything."

And, remembering *everything*, she felt self-conscious and lowered her eyes.

"You're welcome," he said. "Thank *you*."

His voice was husky.

Sarah ventured a glance at him.

Then they both began to laugh, because it seemed crazy to be embarrassed now. Besides, there was so much to talk about. Sarah didn't want to keep her joy all to herself.

"They're bringing the baby," she said. "In just a few minutes."

"I stopped by the nursery while you were sleeping," Steve said. "They've got her all cleaned up and dressed in a T-shirt and diaper and a little pink knit cap. She's adorable. Seven pounds even. Nineteen-and-a-quarter-inches long."

Sarah beamed, so proud. "What was she doing? Was she crying?"

"Sleeping," Steve said. "Worn out, I imagine."

"Mmm," Sarah said. "I hope they don't have to wake her up."

But when the nurse wheeled in the baby in a little glass-sided cart, Alexandra was wide awake and looking around curiously.

The nurse placed her in Sarah's arms, and Sarah was speechless. Thoroughly awed, she could only stare.

The baby blinked large blue eyes and stared back. Then her mouth started making little sucking movements.

The nurse smiled. "You can feed her now. Do you need any help?"

Sarah dragged her gaze away from the soft, round little face. "No," she said. "I think I can manage."

Steve straightened. "I'll leave you two alone for a while."

Sarah didn't protest. She spent the next twenty minutes getting to know her new daughter. Tiny fingers clutched hers as the baby nursed. Sarah could feel the bonding process beginning to happen. It would last a lifetime.

The other nurse came back with the ice and dumped it into Sarah's pitcher.

When she left, Steve came back in, cautiously.

"All done?" he asked, barely poking his head into the room.

"Yes," Sarah said.

"Want company?"

"Absolutely. Come in here, Golden Boy, I'm ready to show off my daughter."

The baby had drifted back to sleep, snug in Sarah's arms.

Steve leaned over the bedside to get a closer look. Love for the two of them swelled and nearly exploded his heart.

"Do you want to hold her?" Sarah asked softly.

Steve drew a breath. "I . . ."

He reached out his arms.

Licked his lips nervously.

"You'll have to coach me through this," he said. "I don't know what I'm doing."

"Nothing to it," Sarah said, carefully placing the blanketed bundle in his large hands. "Just remember to support her neck."

He was shocked to discover that holding Alexandra seemed the most natural thing in the world. She fit perfectly, tiny neck resting in the crook of his elbow, body supported by the length of his forearm.

He had been holding his breath. Now he let it out on a soft chuckle. "It's easy," he said. "It's like she belongs here."

Grinning, he glanced at Sarah and was stabbed by her expression. She was biting her lip, a slight frown worrying her features.

Damn.

This just wasn't fair.

He wanted this baby—wanted the two of them so very, very much.

"Sarah," he said, and felt the stupid sting of salt in his eyes again.

"Steve," she said. "Don't."

Before anything more could be said, Diane Fitzgerald knocked, then entered the room.

Chapter Ten

The blonde was bearing gifts, too, a white coffee mug that said New Mommy and a pink teddy bear with a music box inside.

She wanted to hold the baby, and of course, Steve had to let her. But handing over Alexandra was one of the hardest things he'd ever had to do.

"Support her neck," he said, instructing Diane and watching her carefully.

"All right." The woman was obviously trying to hide a smile.

Sarah laughed. "She's had two of her own," she said. "I think we can trust her with Alexandra."

But you can't trust me, Steve thought bitterly. *After all we've been through together, you can't trust me with your baby or yourself.*

But he guessed he could understand. After all, Sarah had been very badly, very recently hurt. And looking at her, he knew she wasn't going to recover from that for a very long time.

He backed off, leaning against the wall near the door, and watched.

Did Sarah love him? Would staying around and giving her more time be fruitful—or disastrous?

"Hello, Alexandra," Diane cooed, stroking the tiny face. She looked at Sarah. "Alexandra what?" she asked.

Sarah smiled. "Alexandra . . . Diane."

The woman's mouth dropped open, then she beamed, tears forming. "Alexandra Diane," the blonde repeated, smiling down at Sarah's child.

Sarah's child.

Steve could stand it no more.

He had to get out.

Had to get away.

Every minute longer he stayed would only make the final leave-taking more unbearable.

While the two women were laughing and talking and crying and touching Sarah's baby, he took one last, long look, then resolutely slipped out the door.

The hospital rule was that she could keep the baby in the room with her as long as she was awake. And she wanted to be awake—every minute—just so she could keep looking at and touching her baby. She was almost afraid that if she went to sleep, she'd wake up and find that none of it had been real.

Yet her eyes grew heavy.

"I'll call the nursery to come get the baby," Diane said, reaching for the phone. "You've got to rest."

"Don't want to," Sarah mumbled.

"Yes you do," Diane said. "Take advantage of your time here, Sarah. Believe me, you won't get this much opportunity to sleep again for years. Try to enjoy it."

Sarah smiled and reluctantly handed over her baby.

By the time the nurse had taken Alexandra away, Sarah could barely keep her eyes open.

"Go home," she told Diane. "Get some sleep." Then she frowned. "I wonder if that's what Golden Boy's doing. He hasn't been in for at least an hour."

At first he drove in silence—no radio, no tape playing, just the quiet hum of the heater and his thoughts.

His memories.

His hopes and dreams and wishes, all tied up in one beautiful package back in that hospital room.

All pointless and stupid now, in the past.

He had a life to get on with, and that was just what he was going to do.

What he *had* to do.

The only thing he could do.

Twenty minutes outside Chicago, the silence became unbearable.

He jammed an old Jimmy Buffet tape into the player and cranked the volume loud enough to scramble his thoughts.

An hour and a half and he'd be at Claire's....

Claire!

He smacked his forehead and whipped onto the first exit ramp, then found a phone booth.

With all that had happened with Sarah, he'd forgotten to call Claire and tell her he'd been delayed.

His sister had been expecting him since midnight.

The day passed in a pleasant rhythm.

Sarah slept.

Woke.

Called for her baby.

The more rested she got, the more thoroughly she was able to appreciate and enjoy her new daughter.

Every time they brought the baby in, Sarah discovered something different about her. The amazing array of expressions she was capable of—studious frowns, blinking surprise, outraged anger at this new feeling of being hungry even for an instant.

When Sarah talked to her, sang to her, Alexandra gazed directly and seriously into her eyes. Often her tiny fist would grip Sarah's finger with surprising strength.

They were wonderful moments, soft moments, filled with quiet communication, wonder and joy.

For the most part, they were very complete, as well.

Yet there were also times when Sarah felt a stab of longing for someone to share this with. And not just anyone, although she didn't allow herself to pursue that thought to its logical conclusion. It was no use. She'd had time to think and knew that nothing had changed, *could* change, for her, for them.

Sure, she loved him. How could she not? After all they'd been through together...after all he'd been to her. It was natural to feel what she felt for him, wasn't it?

And that was fine, great, except for one thing. What she felt now, what *he* felt now, however strong and genuine, was a thing of the present, born of and nurtured by the circumstances of the parties involved.

It was wonderful and warm and beautiful to love and be loved.

It was not warm and wonderful and beautiful to find that initial love in shattered pieces around your feet.

If there was only herself to consider, maybe she'd do things differently, maybe she'd take the chance. But now there were two who could be hurt by another failure.

Now there was Alexandra.

Remembering her own mother and the endless string of "new loves," Sarah didn't feel that she could take the chance.

Her daughter would have stability, the kind of certainty and security that Sarah had never had.

And the only way she could ensure that was to raise her daughter alone.

Yet . . . as evening approached, even though Diane had returned, Sarah found herself checking the clock, watching the door. And becoming very, very impatient at the absence of one Golden Boy Carlisle.

"I wonder where he is," she said to Diane, frowning. "You'd think if he'd been leaving for the whole day he would've said so."

Diane shrugged and smiled. "Hard telling. Maybe he just meant to take a nap and hasn't woke up yet." Her eyes wandered to the bedside clock, too.

6:30.

Alexandra Diane was almost half a day old.

Steve looked at the mantel clock.

7:15.

Hard to believe that twelve hours ago he had been with Sarah, had witnessed the miracle of new life.

He rubbed his hand over his face and forced his attention back to his sisters, brothers-in-law, nephews and nieces. All had turned out this evening to welcome him home.

Home.

The place where he came to stay for a few days whenever he could. The place where he had a room with his stuff, like some blasted college kid.

He was thirty-five years old.

He wanted a family and home of his own.

"Uncle Steve!" eight-year-old Sherry said, tugging at his arm. "Come see my paintings. I have another one for you."

He smiled and got to his feet. Sherry was a great kid.

As he followed the girl up the stairs, he wondered what talents Alexandra would have. Her mother's sharp mind and ability with words? Her father's ... musical talent....

He slowed on the stairs, feet faltering. Her father. Alexandra's *father*.

While he had heard very briefly about Sarah's ex-husband, the man had never really seemed part of the picture. Probably, he supposed, because Sarah didn't consider him part of the picture.

But now, a child had been born and the father had been nowhere around.

How could he have left them like that?

He clenched his jaw, struggling with the bitter irony of the whole situation. Gary Ramsay had possessed and discarded everything Steve would give his all to have. Sarah and Alexandra. They were both so precious, so special and different. How could any man have treated Sarah and the baby they shared the way Gary Ramsay had? Just turning his back and walking away....

Walking away.

Steve's head came up as the thought sank in.

"Uncle Steve?" Sherry said, looking at him uncertainly. "Are you okay?"

He blinked, cleared his mind.

"Yeah," he said, nodding. "Yeah, Sherry, I think I'm going to be just fine."

9:00 p.m.

Sarah was exhausted.

And hurt.

She hadn't seen or heard from Steve since early that morning.

"You want me to stay tonight?" Diane asked.

"Hmm?" Sarah was still frowning as she forced her attention to Diane. "I'm sorry. What did you say?"

Diane smiled softly. "I said I'm staying with you tonight."

"Oh—no, really. I'm fine. But thanks. You go on home now. You've been here long enough."

"It's no fun to be in a hospital by yourself," Diane said. "Especially if something keeps you from sleeping."

"I won't be by myself," Sarah said. "I can have Alexandra any time I want her. If I can't sleep, I'll call for her, and my daughter and I will have a great time together. Really, Diane. Go home. See your own family. Besides—" her lips hardened into a line "—there's nothing that's going to keep me from sleeping. I'm so tired, nothing in the world—"

"You're upset," Diane said, leaning forward in the gold-vinyl chair next to Sarah's bed. "Admit it. You want Steve to be here and you're upset."

"I'm not," she insisted, raising her chin. "Steven Carlisle can be anywhere he wants to, anytime. What he does is none of my business."

"Only because you made it that way." Diane leaned her elbows on her knees. "He told me, you know. Earlier."

Sarah's eyes grew wary. "Told you what?"

Diane shrugged. "That you weren't interested in him...romantically—as anything other than as a friend."

Sarah licked her lips. "I'm not."

"Bull."

"No." Sarah shook her head. "I'm not. Diane, I'm not interested in *anybody* right now. Not *that* way. Not—"

"Maybe I used the wrong word," Diane said. "Maybe I should have said *love*."

"Same thing," Sarah said, but knew it wasn't. Romance was one thing, and she really *hadn't* been interested in romance for many months. Romance called up images of flowers and candy and dating and electric kisses. But love . . . love was different.

Love was kindness and caring and being there when things weren't fun and she didn't look pretty. Like last night. Love was solid and dependable and secure, something you knew you could count on when you needed it. With Gary, she had had shallow romance. With Steve, she had had . . . love.

"I think—" Diane stopped, cleared her throat and went on. "Sarah . . . maybe I shouldn't say this to you right now. Maybe I shouldn't bring it up."

Sarah frowned. "But . . . ?"

Diane took a deep breath, let it out. "But . . . I think Steve is gone."

Sarah blinked, then narrowed her eyes. "Gone? What do you mean, 'gone'?"

"I don't know. I may be wrong. But I just . . . I don't know. I think he might have gone back to New York."

Sarah froze.

Stared.

Remembered.

She remembered now why he'd come back to the apartment last night.

To say goodbye.

Last night he'd been packed and on his way out of town.

"No." It was a whispered sound, which she was barely aware of making. "No." She shook her head. "Diane, he wouldn't do that. He wouldn't leave without saying goodbye."

Diane bit her lip, then smiled. "You're probably right."

But in that instant, Sarah knew she was very, very wrong.

He was driving too fast and got a ticket, which slowed him down.

It was 10:35 p.m. when he finally turned the car into the hospital parking lot.

The front doors were locked and he had to go through Emergency to get in. He took the elevator up to the fourth floor.

His heart was beating a mile a minute and his palms were slick with sweat. He got out of the elevator and had to remind himself that nothing had changed. Sarah felt no differently. She didn't know that he had gone through the agony of saying goodbye for good and then changed his mind, listened to his heart.

He was back in Chicago to stay.

It probably wasn't smart.

It definitely wouldn't be easy, with Sarah's determination to keep him out.

But, he reminded himself again as he headed down the long hall, it would be worth it. Just to be close, to be her friend, to share whatever parts of her life and herself that she would allow. To catch glimpses of Alexandra as she grew and changed.

If he had learned anything this day, it was that you cannot walk away from those you love. At least he couldn't. And instead of playing an all-or-nothing game, he'd just have to take what he could get. And give what she would take.

He paused outside her room. Wiped his hands on his jeans. Tapped lightly on the half-closed door and wondered if she was asleep.

"Come in?" Sarah said.

The room was dark, except for the blue glow of the TV. The picture was on, but the volume was off. Distant, muted bells sounded from the elevators and nurse's station, and the heating system thrummed.

"Steve," Sarah said.

"Hi."

"Hi." Her face was blank and he wondered if she could read the changes within him and hoped she could not.

If this was to work—and it *had* to work—he had to bury his feelings for her instead of letting them out every time he felt like it. It would get easier with time, he was sure. But right now, right this minute, he loved her so much that he felt like it was oozing out his pores. It seemed a year since he had seen her.

"How are you?" he asked.

"Fine," she answered, still looking at him with that unreadable stare.

He grinned and shoved his hands into his pockets. He should have waited till morning to come see her, waited till he'd had time to gear himself for their new relationship and to plan how to rebuild the old one.

"And the baby," he said, "how's she?"

Sarah nodded. "Fine. She's fine."

"I hope I'm not too late," he said. "If you want me to go, I'll go—"

"No." She finally looked away, then back. "No. I'm glad you came. I thought—"

"What?" he asked.

She shrugged, smiled and shook her dark head. "Nothing. Never mind." She gestured to a chair. "Sit down, Steve. I was just about to call for the baby."

It was so *good* to have him here, Sarah thought, her throat aching with the tears she'd been trying not to shed ever since he'd walked through the door. Why did it have to be so darned *good*?

He held Alexandra the way he'd handle a priceless, fragile treasure. But there was no fear in the way he handled her, no anxiety. Just care and delicacy...love. Firmness and strength. Joy.

His expression—that gentle smile as he talked to the baby—melted Sarah's heart.

Alexandra gazed raptly into his mint-green, smiling eyes. She clutched his big fingers and snuggled up against his chest.

He loves her, Sarah thought. *And she knows it. More importantly, I know it. I would trust my daughter's very life with this man....*

"I—I thought you were gone," she said, and heard the quiver in her voice.

Steve looked at her for a long moment. "I was at my sister's."

"Oh."

"I had some thinking to do," he said. "About my future."

"Oh?"

He nodded. Grinned. Carefully wrapped Alexandra's blanket more snugly around her. "I'm getting old, Sarah. Too old to be trotting around the world and living out of a suitcase. I've decided to settle down—get a real job. A house. A car. Maybe a dog. You know, all the dull stuff people do when they think about turning forty."

"I see. Well, uh, just where are you going to do all this dull stuff? New York?"

He leaned back in the chair. "I'm from this area originally. All my family is here, within a couple hours of Chicago."

"So you're going to live here." Sarah couldn't control the little flutter of her heart. He'd been absent from her life for only one day and that had been enough. When she'd thought he'd gone for good . . .

But he was back. He was staying.

She smiled. "That's nice. I'm sure your sisters are pleased."

He laughed. "Oh, yeah. Pleased and shocked. And anxious. They've all volunteered to come up and help me house hunt right away. I think they want to see me sign a mortgage and buy furniture before I change my mind."

"But you won't," Sarah said.

"No. I won't."

"You sound so sure."

"I'm committed."

Something in his voice tugged at her. She swallowed and found it suddenly hard to breathe.

Was he staying because of her?

Crazy! she thought. He knew they had no future.

In fact, something about him seemed to have changed drastically in the hours since she'd last seen him. When she searched his face, she saw no signs of the emotion that had been there before. Had it been a passing thing? Or had she hurt him so much by rejections that it didn't really matter anymore?

So fast. His feelings for her had changed so fast.

Why wasn't she elated to see that the blatant love was gone from his eyes?

Why did she feel so... hurt. So... disappointed. So... suddenly lost and alone.

What she saw in him now was a warm and caring friendship—exactly what she said, *thought* she wanted. And was shaken by the sense of bitter betrayal it provoked.

"Well," she said, lifting her chin. "I'm glad you're doing something that makes you happy."

He looked down at Alexandra, who had fallen asleep. "I am," he said. "I need this. I need some stability in my life."

Not *I need to be near you.* Not *I love you and found I couldn't bear to leave.* Just, *I need some stability in my life.* Which was, of course, what she had represented to him all along.

She'd known it. Known it was too good to be true. Too good to last.

His undying devotion to her hadn't even lasted twenty-four hours.

Well, that was just damned fine with her. But she had news for him. Stability wasn't going to fill the void he was feeling. Neither was some stupid house or car or job. He needed *people*, damn it! People who loved him and needed him and made his life worthwhile.

What he needed was someone like her—and someone like Alexandra.

And blast it all, she thought, looking at him, feeling the tears finally break through, she and Alexandra needed someone like him.

Not someone.

Him.

"Sarah?" he said, his voice full of concern. "What's wrong? Do you want me to call the nurse?"

"No." She shook her head. "No. I want you to leave. I want you to get out of here right now and go find yourself a house and a car and a dog. Just go! Go find yourself whatever is going to make you happy."

He frowned. "Sarah. What—"

"Go!" she demanded, knowing she was really losing it. Why had she had to fall in love with him? Her life had been going so well. She could have been moderately happy, moderately content. And now?

There would always be something missing.

"Calm down," he said. "If you want me to go, I'll go. Just let me call the nurse to come get Alexandra."

"Give her to me." She reached for the baby.

"You'll upset her," he said, but didn't try to keep Sarah from taking her.

She paused, knowing he was right. Babies knew when something was wrong.

"Then call," she said. "Now."

He did. They waited in silence for a minute.

"I'm sorry I upset you. If I had known it would be like this, I wouldn't have come here tonight."

"Why did you?" Sarah asked.

"Because I wanted to see you, both of you."

"Why?"

"Why?" He frowned. "You know why. Because I care about you. Sarah, we went through something very special together last night. I'll never forget it. It's something that will always kind of tie us together, don't you think?"

"As friends?" Sarah asked bitterly.

He held her gaze, then nodded slowly, very seriously. "Yes. As friends. I hope we'll always be that."

That was the final straw. An admission that his feelings had changed—or, more accurately, had been misunderstood by him before, just as she'd known.

A bitter smile curved her mouth. "That's funny, Golden Boy. That's supposed to be my line."

"What do you mean? Sarah, what is going on with you?"

She shrugged, wiped her eyes, straightened her shoulders. "Last night I told you that you had just gotten caught up in everything—me, the baby, domestic stuff. You insisted that that wasn't it, that you were just *so* in love with me." She laughed. "You see, I was right all along. If you'd just listened to me, all of the awkward moments we've been through in the past twenty-four hours could have been spared."

He was staring at her, clearly bewildered. She sniffled and he handed her a tissue.

"What are you saying?" he asked.

"Nothing." She shook her head. "Just...nothing. I'm tired, Steve."

"You're angry." He studied her. "You don't want me to stay in Chicago, do you?"

She shrugged, dying inside. "What you do is none of my business."

"But you don't want me here."

"I don't care."

He nodded slowly. "Well, that's terrific. Because I care a whole hell of a lot about you. I suppose you're going to be furious when you find out where I'm going to work."

She lifted her chin warily. "Not Houston's..."

"Yes, Houston's."

No, Sarah thought, as he went on to explain about Mark's offer. *No.*

She couldn't work with this man, not now. Not knowing how she felt about him and knowing how he truly felt about her. He cared about her like he cared about one of his sisters. She'd given him every chance to deny it, to restate his so-called love.

He was watching her, waiting for her response to his announcement.

"That's nice," she said tightly. "Where is that nurse? Call them again. I'm really very tired." And that was true. She felt drained of everything—feelings, energy, everything. All she wanted right now was to have him gone.

"Sarah." He was frowning. "Obviously you hate the idea of working with me. If it's because of...what I said last night and you think I'm going to make things awkward, you don't have to worry. You've made your feelings very clear, and I will respect that."

"That's very generous of you. Call the nursery."

"You don't believe me."

She forced herself to look at him. "Oh, I believe you. Don't worry, I haven't got the faintest delusion that you're staying because of some grand passion for me. I'm not concerned that you'll spend your days at Houston's chasing me around the desk or something."

"Then what?" he asked. "What is it?"

"Nothing. I'm really too tired to talk. It's been a big day and—"

"Why are you angry with me?" he asked, his voice low but incredibly intense. "What have I done?"

She lowered her eyes, sank back against the pillows.

"Nothing," she said softly. "Really, Steve. You haven't done anything. I guess I'm just...angry at myself."

For hoping, for believing, for succumbing for even a moment to the idea that a future together could actually be more than just pretty, impossible fiction.

"You're regretting asking me to stay last night," Steve said, and seemed hurt by it.

"No," she said. "Yes. I don't know. I'm a little mixed up."

"You're afraid that what we went through last night and this morning has ruined our...friendship."

She stared at her hands, decided she owed him at least partial honesty. "Yes."

"Damn," he said softly. "I knew you'd regret it. I told Diane that this morning. Look, Sarah. Nothing's changed unless we let it change."

She began to cry again, tears falling softly, because everything had changed. *She* had changed, so much more than she'd ever thought possible. She wanted him so much. Needed him so much. She, who hadn't needed anyone since childhood.

"Sarah," he said, touching her arm. "Please talk to me."

She didn't pull away and he moved to sit on the bed, Alexandra still sleeping peacefully in the cradle of one strong arm.

Why couldn't it be like this? Sarah cried inside. Why couldn't it be the three of them, together like this. Touching, sharing, loving...

"Mrs. Jordan?" the nurse said, coming into the room. "I'm here for the baby."

"No," Sarah said. "I've changed my mind. I want her here for a while."

As the nurse left, Steve said, "I thought you were tired."

"I am."

His fingers found hers, tangling warmly together. "Whatever is bothering you, Sarah, don't let it. Everything will work out, you'll see. We'll make it work out—together. Whatever you want, I want you to tell me. If it's within my power, I'll do it, you know that. You have to know that. I just... I just want you and Alexandra to be happy."

She raised her eyes to meet his. Felt the warmth of his hand, the comfort of his nearness. Saw something in his eyes, heard something in his voice that gave her hope.

"You mean that?" she asked.

"With everything I have in me. What do you want, Sarah? What would make you happy?"

She bit her lip, and had never been so scared of making a fool of herself in her life.

But looking at him, she knew she had to take the chance.

"It would make me happy if my daughter had a—" She faltered, had to swallow.

"A what?" he asked, smiling encouragement. "Gold-plated baby bed? Private zoo? Olympic-size swimming pool?"

Sarah laughed. He had always, always been able to make her laugh.

Then she sobered and prayed for the guts to follow through.

"No...actually, I was thinking along the lines of a—a father." The last two words came out in a rush.

Steve blinked, showing no expression. "I don't understand."

"Well, it's silly, I know. It's just that you seem so...taken with her, I just thought. Never mind. Forget I said—"

Her words were cut off by a kiss—the sweetest, warmest, most beautiful kiss she had ever experienced in her life.

It lasted and lasted, going through stages of rising excitement and gentle exploration.

Sarah was crying, but that didn't stop anything.

Hugged between them, Alexandra began to squirm.

Steve pulled away, and there were tears in his eyes, too. "I love you so much," he said.

"We love you, too."

Eventually, Sarah moved over in the bed and Steve climbed in beside her. Alexandra was between them and seemed very content and happy to be there.

They stayed there, together, all night. A family. And knew that this first night was only the beginning of so many wonderful nights and days to come.

* * *

The next morning, Steve made some calls. Six, actually. To each of his sisters, announcing that he was getting married.

"And that's not all," he said, one arm around Sarah and one hand resting on the beautiful little girl in her arms. "I also called to tell you that I have just become a father. Seven pounds, even. Nineteen-and-a-quarter-inches long. And she's got the biggest, most beautiful blue eyes and this little tiny button of a nose and . . ."

Beside him, Sarah smiled. And loved. So much that she would never have believed it possible.

Only in fiction?

Oh, no. Only with the most absolutely *right* man.

Under those circumstances, she had begun to believe that virtually anything was possible.

* * * * *

COMING NEXT MONTH

#724 CIMARRON KNIGHT—Pepper Adams
A Diamond Jubilee Book!
Single mom Noelle Chandler thought she didn't need a knight in
shining armor. Then sexy rancher Brody Sawyer rode into her life.
This is Book #1 of the *Cimarron Stories*.

#725 FEARLESS FATHER—Terry Essig
Absent-minded Jay Gand fearlessly tackled a temporary job of
parenting. After all, how hard could it be? Then he found out, and
without neighbor Catherine Escabito he would never have survived!

#726 FAITH, HOPE AND LOVE—Geeta Kingsley
Luke Summers's ardent pursuit of romance-shy Rachel Carstairs was
met with cool indifference. But Luke was determined to fill the lovely
loner's heart with faith, hope...and his love.

#727 A SEASON FOR HOMECOMING—Laurie Paige
Book I of HOMEWARD BOUND DUO
Their ill-fated love had sent Lainie Alder away from Devlin Garrick—
and her home—years ago. Now, Dev needed her back. Would her
homecoming fulfill broken promises of the past?

#728 FAMILY MAN—Arlene James
Weston Caudell's love for his estranged nephew warmed wary Joy
Morrow, but would the handsome businessman leave as quickly as
he'd come—with her beloved charge...and her heart?

#729 THE SEDUCTION OF ANNA—Brittany Young
Dynamic country doctor Esteban Alvarado set his sights on Anna
Bennett, but her well-ordered life required she resist him. Yet Anna
hadn't counted on Esteban's slow, sweet seduction....

AVAILABLE THIS MONTH:

 *Silhouette Romance*®

DIAMOND JUBILEE
CELEBRATION!

It's the Silhouette Books tenth anniversary, and what better way to celebrate than to toast *you*, our readers, for making it all possible. Each month in 1990 we'll present you with a DIAMOND JUBILEE Silhouette Romance written by an all-time favorite author! Saying thanks has never been so romantic...

The merry month of May will bring you SECOND TIME LUCKY by Victoria Glenn. And in June, the first volume of Pepper Adams's exciting trilogy Cimarron Stories will be available—CIMARRON KNIGHT. July sizzles with BORROWED BABY by Marie Ferrarella. Suzanne Carey, Lucy Gordon, Annette Broadrick and many more have special gifts of love waiting for you with their DIAMOND JUBILEE Romances.

You'll flip . . . your pages won't!
Read paperbacks *hands-free* with

Book Mate•I

The perfect "mate" for all your romance paperbacks

**Traveling • Vacationing • At Work • In Bed • Studying
• Cooking • Eating**

Perfect size for all standard paperbacks, this wonderful invention makes reading a pure pleasure! Ingenious design holds paperback books OPEN and FLAT so even wind can't ruffle pages – leaves your hands free to do other things. Reinforced, wipe-clean vinyl-covered holder flexes to let you turn pages without undoing the strap . . . supports paperbacks so well, they have the strength of hardcovers!

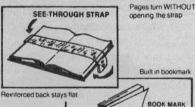

Pages turn WITHOUT opening the strap

SEE-THROUGH STRAP

Reinforced back stays flat

Built in bookmark

BOOK MARK

BACK COVER HOLDING STRIP

10 x 7¼ opened
Snaps closed for easy carrying, too

A duo by Laurie Paige

There's no place like home—and Laurie Paige's delightful duo captures that heartwarming feeling in two special stories set in Arizona ranchland. Share the poignant homecomings of two lovely heroines—half sisters Lainie and Tess—as they travel on the road to romance with their rugged, handsome heroes.

A SEASON FOR HOMECOMING—Lainie and Dev's story…coming in June.

HOME FIRES BURNING BRIGHT—Tess and Carson's story…coming in July.

Come home to A SEASON FOR HOMECOMING and HOME FIRES BURNING BRIGHT…only from Silhouette Romance!